BLOOD TRAIL

A KYLE PAYNE THRILLER

JT SAWYER

INKUBATOR
BOOKS

Published by Inkubator Books

www.inkubatorbooks.com

Copyright © 2025 by JT Sawyer

JT Sawyer has asserted his right to be identified as the author of this work.

ISBN (eBook): 978-1-83756-535-1
ISBN (Paperback): 978-1-83756-536-8
ISBN (Hardback): 978-1-83756-537-5

PROLOGUE
ABSYNTH, NORTHERN CALIFORNIA

If Aaron Daly had known his last day on Earth would end with three hollow-point rounds to the stomach, he would have reined in his curiosity.

But his scientific mind could hardly be squelched, and it was what led him to revisiting a meadow west of his hometown. Aaron had to confirm his suspicions that the Wayland Corporation's agricultural research facility was propagating a particular type of beetle in their eighty-acre grain fields.

But why? It just doesn't make sense. It's not even possible for the beetle to survive outside of its native habitat.

He slowed his Nissan pickup along the two-lane highway and made a left turn onto a dirt road with lush weeds growing out of the cracked earth. A half mile later, the road ended, and he parked.

Aaron checked his iPhone one last time to see if his sister had answered this morning's text, but there was no response. He stared at the screen image of him and Eva from when they last met, a smile sliding over his face.

Always in some far-flung place across the globe when I need you the most.

He slid the phone into the cargo pocket on his tan pants and grabbed his daypack from the rear bench seat of his truck. After locking his rig, he moved down a slope just beyond his vehicle and followed the red clay shoreline of a meandering creek for ten minutes, pausing every fifty feet or so to scan his surroundings for anyone following him.

Technically, this region was part of Klamath National Forest, but that would soon change to private property in another three hundred yards.

The sun was streaming through the conifer branches that lined the creek. He marveled at the old leviathans, which had escaped the lumbermen's saws a hundred years earlier when Northern California forests were being harvested for their redwoods, cedars and pines.

A few minutes later, he climbed out of the creek bed and moved through the knee-high bushes for thirty feet before stopping at a transition zone where the forest ended and a large meadow began.

He gazed at the undulating waves of wheat blowing softly in the wind beyond the twelve-foot-high barbed-wire fence just a stone's throw away. The agro-site extended over much of the southern edge of Wayland's eighty-acre property, and this particular patch of cereal crops was nearing harvest time.

He waited and watched, forcing himself to be patient, continually scanning the nearest perimeter camera until it rotated in the other direction. Then he made his move.

Aaron darted for the corner fence post on his right, squatting down directly below the camera, which was panned up.

He removed his daypack, unzipping the front compartment, which contained a glass tube with a cork top and a botanical plant press kit.

He didn't have to search very hard to find his test subjects. The stalks of wheat pressing against and through the chain-link fence were rife with the pest beetles. Some of them were crawling over other beetles to get to a new sprig of food. He bent down a stalk, flicking several of the pea-sized insects into his collection tube, then corked the top.

Aaron held up the vial to the sun, studying his new captives to make sure they met his needs.

Just like the ones I found last week with the odd white splotches on their exoskeletons. What the hell are you beetles doing in my country?

He slid the vial into his pack and grabbed several of the shin-high wheat stalks, twisting them until the roots broke free from the rich black soil. These he carefully placed flat inside the plant press, which resembled an oversized book with a wooden front and back.

His head snapped to the left. It sounded like a herd of deer bounding towards him.

Until he saw that it wasn't.

Three men in gray security guard uniforms were trotting through the meadow with their pistols extended.

He felt his stomach lurch into his throat when the first bullets ricocheted off the metal fence post beside him.

Shit, this place must have a secret to protect just like I thought.

Aaron slung the pack on his shoulder and tucked the plant press under his left arm, bounding for the woods and scurrying down the slope into the creek bed.

His return route wasn't nearly as graceful or methodical, especially with the trees around him splintering apart from gunfire. He bolted forty feet, only to trip and fall in the creek, then get up and repeat the process until he had retraced his steps back to the jumping-off point.

The gunshots had stopped. He slowly climbed up the slope, peering above the edge at his truck in the distance.

You got this.

He took several lunge steps up to the forest floor, feeling his boots on firm ground. The punch in his gut felt like a hot metal spike had been driven through him. Two more followed, his abdomen feeling like someone had just sunk a pitchfork into his innards.

Aaron dropped the plant press, holding his hands against the leaking bullet holes in his torso. It was then that he recalled the piercing sound of gunshots. It was so surreal. None of it was like the movies he'd watched over the years. He wasn't propelled back into the creek bed, nor did his body ripple with electrical movement.

He simply couldn't move, his life force trickling past his fingers. And despite his desperate attempt to stem the bleeding, he knew the sand in his hourglass had just been reduced to a few grains.

He fell to his knees, fumbling in his side pocket and removing his phone. All he could think about was desperately wanting to speak with his sister.

"Aaron Daly," said a disembodied voice beyond his truck.

He looked up at the big man in a faded green T-shirt and jeans walking towards him. The guy's use of his name seemed to evoke a question more than a statement.

"You?" Aaron bleated out as he fought to breathe.

"You shouldn'ta been pokin' around here." A large Rottweiler with a gold choke collar bared its teeth and was about to pounce, but the man commanded the dog to sit.

Aaron slumped to his side, blood spooling from his trembling lips. "Whatever you're doing out here with Wayland, it goes...goes far beyond this town, and if I'm right, even beyond our...our shores."

"I really don't care." The large man tucked his pistol into his beltline, leaning over Aaron. "You'd better hope that what you uncovered dies with you, or there are gonna be a lot of backwoods graves around Absynth."

Aaron gasped his final breath, a grimace forming as he gazed at the image of Eva on his phone.

CHAPTER 1
WEAVERVILLE, NORTHERN CALIFORNIA

Kyle Payne removed the gas nozzle from his Indian motorcycle, then screwed the cap back on the tank. He headed across the lot and into the store to use the restroom and buy a cup of black coffee.

He was ready for this day of travel to be over. Though the sights along the way had been spectacular, he was looking forward to sacking out in his hammock at the campsite forty miles up the road. The past few months of leisurely travel up the California coast had seen him staying at a new campground nearly every night as he explored the mountains, deserts and quaint towns dotting the diverse countryside. With only one more week left in California, Payne was looking forward to pushing up along the Oregon coast.

After paying for his coffee, he stepped outside, standing in the shade near the ice freezers and observing local life. He heard some laughter around the corner and stepped closer, peering around the side. A thin man with a wispy goatee and black hair was sitting on the curb, tossing popcorn to some pigeons. Half of the birds were teetering as they walked, their balance clearly affected, while the rest were lying on their sides.

The man took a swig from his beer bottle, then poured some on the popcorn in his other hand before tossing the treats to the birds. He watched the pigeons gobble up the morsels; then he let out a raucous laugh as the birds struggled to stay upright.

Payne stepped closer. "You might find that funny as hell, but their tiny livers can't handle alcohol. You're gonna kill 'em if you keep that up."

The man canted his head, his smile fading. He removed another handful of popcorn from the bag beside his leg and poured a copious amount of beer on it before flinging it in the parking lot.

Payne set his coffee down on the curb and rushed at the approaching swarm of birds, waving them off.

The man stood. "What the hell's the matter with you? You some kinda nature freak?"

Payne stepped closer. He was at least a foot taller than the scraggly figure, whose yellow teeth were showing beyond his inebriated grin.

"You want a piece of me, tough guy?" said the man.

"Doesn't look like there are too many pieces to you, actually."

"Fuck you, man," he shouted, waving the popcorn bag in the air before dumping the remaining food on the ground.

"Hey, Merle, we should go," said someone near the back of the parking lot. Payne saw a burly man in a leather vest leaning out the window of a white van.

"Yeah, yeah," said the drunk guy near Payne. He crumpled the white bag and tossed it at Payne's feet, then meandered towards the vehicle. The van slowly drove off and disappeared around the corner.

Payne bent over and picked up the most inebriated

pigeons and walked over to a large pine tree, placing them in the shade. When he finished, he grabbed an old broom leaning against the back door and swept up the popcorn, tossing it in the trash.

After he finished his coffee, he drove through downtown and headed north on Highway 3.

———

THE NEXT MORNING, they came for Payne at his campsite while he was only half awake and enjoying the aroma of coffee simmering on his portable stove. He had barely lifted the spoon of steaming oatmeal to his lips when two officers swept in from the trail along the side of his site.

Not even the jays in the trees squawked, and he surmised that the officers had waited for a gust of wind to cloak their steps along the leaf-strewn path before blitzing into view.

From their two-tone tan uniforms, he could see they were deputies and not state police. Not that it would have mattered.

The man and woman moved with purpose, and the intensity in their eyes came from an admixture of adrenaline laced with fear. With their Sig P226 pistols leveled at him, he knew they were certain they had gotten their man.

Payne oscillated between feelings of shock and outrage. He could see the man's hands trembling slightly. It didn't help that the deputy had his finger on the pistol trigger, making Payne wonder how often the man had utilized the weapon.

Sloppy as hell. You just get out of the academy?

The woman had her index finger extended above the trigger and alternated glances between Payne and her immediate surroundings like someone accustomed to situational awareness.

So she's running the show.

"Hands behind your back," shouted the man, who stopped ten feet to Payne's right, while the female deputy moved past her partner and faced Payne head-on across the picnic table. "Now," he snapped, with his teeth bared.

Payne set his hand-carved spoon down and placed both hands flat on the table. "You wanna tell me what this is about?"

"Homicide, asshole, that's what. Found the dude you killed in his vehicle a half mile from here." The deputy appeared to be in his late twenties with bristly blond hair and fierce blue eyes. He really wanted this arrest, and Payne wondered if the man was trying to make an impression on the woman, whose body language belied a confidence unfamiliar to her associate.

"Easy, John," said the woman as she fired a glance at her partner. "Just cuff him while I keep him covered."

Payne glanced beyond her shoulder at the empty campground. He had specifically chosen this place because it was small, and being it was midweek, he figured the place would be quiet. He had enjoyed a peaceful night of rest in his hammock, but only the chipmunks could confirm any of that, and Payne knew he was, no doubt, bound for whichever town the county jail was located in.

And a round of questioning about the death of whomever he supposedly killed.

He ran through his options. Given his background, his training told him he could fight, flee or surrender. He had no intention of the latter two, and attempting disarming moves would certainly reinforce his guilt status and turn him into the subject of a manhunt afterwards.

Payne wished he had stowed the .38 Smith and Wesson snubbie revolver in the pannier on his Indian motorcycle. Instead, it sat in a fanny pack on the bench beside him, which was only going to add to his dilemma. Given California's nonpermissive gun laws, he kept it concealed, and it only served as a backup tool in case he broke down on the highway, or for security while sleeping in the boonies.

Payne placed his hands behind his back like the deputy requested, before having the cuffs cinched in place. He was hoisted up by his right arm. He slid his legs out from under the table and stood while the deputy read him his rights, stuttering on a few words.

Payne glanced at the man's polished name tag. *Deputy Kessel.*

The man removed the Spyderco folding knife clipped inside Payne's front pants pocket and placed it in his vest.

The woman moved towards the table, easing one hand off her pistol and using her other to turn off the stove. She grabbed the fanny pack and unzipped the main compartment, glancing inside. Her eyes narrowed. "You got a permit for this firearm, sir?"

Payne felt his gut sink. "No. I don't. I only carry that because I'm usually camping in the woods a lot."

"You sure?" said Kessel as he gazed at his partner. "That has to be the murder weapon."

"We'll see," she said. Now that she was closer, he could read her bronze nameplate, *Deputy Monroe.*

"It's a felony offense to have a firearm without a permit outside of your residence, dumbass," muttered Kessel as he clutched Payne's arm tighter.

"Like I said, I only carry it because I'm on the road, and the ballistics tests I'm sure you're going to run are gonna tell you it hasn't been fired recently."

Monroe zipped up the pack and slung it over her shoulder. She walked to the motorcycle, flipping up the unlocked pannier tops on both sides and glancing through the interiors. When she finished, she gazed at the hammock strung between the two trees on the edge of the campsite. "Been here long?" she asked.

"Drove down from Lassen National Park yesterday evening. I'm taking a field course on animal tracking this weekend with an instructor named Tommy Larkin, so I was planning to camp here for a few nights."

"And then plugged a guy full of holes before calling it a night, am I right?" asked Kessel.

"You seem to already have your investigation wrapped up, so why keep asking me questions?" inquired Payne.

Monroe waved her pistol towards the road. "Let's get him back to the station and process him."

"Don't suppose it matters if I tell you I'm not your guy?" he asked as the three of them walked down the gravel road towards the entrance.

"We got a call, mister," said the man who kept a viselike grip on Payne's right elbow. "Said someone fitting your description was seen running from the crime scene toward the campground this morning."

"The victim was shot in the abdomen multiple times," said the woman, who hung back a few feet to Payne's left with her gun held at her side.

"And you think I was running back here to grab a bowl of oatmeal with raisins and brown sugar before leisurely packing up my camp and heading out?"

The man shoved Payne along the road. "I didn't do it. I'm innocent. I was set up," Kessel muttered in a sarcastic tone. "Save it, pal. I've heard it before."

Payne was having a hard time containing his frustration, which was now turning to a simmering fury. "You mean on the training videos at the academy."

"Just pipe down," said the woman. "We'll be at the station in Absynth in thirty minutes, and you can give us your side of the story then, or lawyer up, should you choose." Despite her attempt to sound detached, he sensed some irritation in her voice like she had been jarred from a deep sleep to investigate the bogus phone call.

Who would have pointed a finger at me for killing someone? There hasn't been anyone else at this campground, and I only encountered a few folks in the other towns on the drive in yesterday.

He thought about the crackhead feeding the pigeons but dismissed him since he'd had no one follow him during the forty-mile drive north. *Plus, the drunken birds rivaled that guy's IQ.*

They rounded the bend near the entrance and continued on the blacktop road for a few minutes, eventually stopping at the parked police cruiser pulled onto the shoulder. It was a black Dodge Charger whose doors were pinstriped with hundreds of scratches from probably driving off road in a vehicle that wasn't meant for such abuse.

As the woman opened the back door, Payne glanced back over his shoulder. "What about all my gear and my bike?"

"Least of your worries, man," said Kessel. "Like I said, you're under arrest for murder and felony possession of a firearm. You should think long and hard about all that."

As he got into the back seat, Payne didn't have to ruminate for very long. *I haven't killed anyone, lately.*

CHAPTER 2

THE DRIVE BACK TO ABSYNTH TOOK A LITTLE OVER THIRTY minutes since the two deputies stopped at the crime scene a half mile east of the campground.

Deputy Monroe pulled the Charger between a black van with the Absynth County logo on it and a blue Nissan pickup where two men in white bio-suits were gathering evidence from the interior. The older man had a black beard that crept out from his mask as he directed the younger forensics analyst, who was busy taking photographs.

The passenger door of the Nissan was ajar, revealing a pasty corpse with swollen lips and glassy eyes that had drawn the attention of every fly in California. The guy's face resembled raw hamburger and looked like it had been dragged for a mile over volcanic rock.

Payne could see three bullet wounds in the abdomen, which revealed the grisly damage typical of hollow-point rounds from a pistol.

Shot from the front. 9 mm, most likely. Took him a few minutes to die from being gutshot like that. Helluva way to go.

Monroe and Kessel exited the Charger, remaining near the cruiser while Monroe addressed the older man.

Payne only caught snippets of the conversation through the window but enough to know that the bruising on the dead guy's arms indicated he had been dragged by someone and placed in the vehicle.

After the tech had completed his photography assignment, he slung the Nikon over his shoulder and helped his boss remove the body from the vehicle, placing it on an open body bag on the ground.

Payne noticed three things: the first was that the corpse was semi-rigid, which told him that the man hadn't died during the past few hours, as Deputy Kessel had indicated.

The second was that the color seemed to drain from Monroe's face. Payne questioned if she was as experienced an officer as he first thought given how it seemed like she was about to pass out at the sight of the bloated corpse.

The third was more interesting. The dead guy's boots had traces of red clay on the treads. Payne glanced at the ground in the forest beyond the vehicles; he looked to his right at a muddy drainage by a culvert that cut under the road, then to a narrow game trail that wound through the ferns on the opposite side of the road. Black soil or mud, just like he'd seen at the campground and everywhere else around the region.

The tracker in him was curious and filed the observation away. Not that it probably mattered. He had planned on staying in the region until Monday, but now he wanted to leave this place in his rearview mirror. It seemed like that hope was about to be dashed, and his new home for the time being was going to be a cell in Absynth.

———

AFTER ARRIVING IN TOWN, Deputy Monroe escorted Payne into the lobby of the sheriff's station, past a redheaded secretary sitting at the front desk and towards one of the three temporary holding cells against the left wall.

Absynth was new to him. After leaving Lassen Volcanic National Park yesterday, he'd driven west through Redding, then up to Weaverville, before heading north on Highway 3, through a bunch of towns with only stop signs, which made the two-mile-long strip of trinket shops and restaurants in Absynth seem like a mecca.

Monroe nudged Payne inside the ten-by-ten compartment, then closed the self-locking door while she remained outside the cell. She had him turn around to remove the cuffs through the bars, then had him swivel towards her, repositioning them at his front.

His options were to stand or take a seat on the bed bolted to the floor. He sat and studied his surroundings while Monroe discussed the morning events with the secretary, who was addressed as Dottie.

A few minutes later, an older man emerged from a room down the hallway. The sixty-something figure walked with a limp, his cowboy boots clacking on the faded tiles. By his pasty complexion and gaunt face, Payne wondered if the guy had early onset rigor mortis. The lawman paused before the holding cell, observing Payne like a spectator at the zoo.

A tarnished sheriff's badge was above the left breast pocket of his uniform, and the man sported a 1911 pistol in a leather holster on his right hip.

Payne glanced beyond the man to the four framed photos on the wall, which showed the two deputies, the secretary, and the sheriff, whose name was listed below as Jerry Hanson.

"Give you any trouble?" Hanson said over his shoulder to Monroe.

"No, actually. Calm as can be. Was eatin' oatmeal at a picnic table without a care in the world when we pulled up."

"Well, he fits the description I got earlier. Time will tell if he's the son of a bitch who killed that fella along the road."

"Kessel stayed back with the forensics team at the crime scene. He's going to take them to the campsite afterwards and survey the rest of the guy's things before heading back here."

Payne leaned forward, resting his cuffed hands on his knees. "Like I already told your deputies, I'm out this way to attend a class with Tommy Larkin at the Daly Field Institute up the road. You really think I'd be camping a half mile away from a dead guy if I had been behind his murder?"

The sheriff rolled his tongue around his teeth like he had something stuck. "Seen stranger things in my day. Plus, I got a call saying you, or someone exactly like you, was seen running down the road away from the victim's truck."

"Who made the call?"

"Um, hang on while I get the name and address for you." He narrowed his eyes. "Just sit there and shut the hell up."

Monroe moved up alongside her boss, holding up Payne's driver's license. "Guy's name is Kyle Payne out of Alexandria, Virginia. Said he arrived in the area yesterday evening. Rolled in on a pretty slick motorcycle."

"Biker, eh?" The statement was loaded, and the man's eyes lingered over Payne's beard and face for a moment before he turned and walked over to the coffee machine behind the front desk. He removed an overturned mug and poured it full, then glanced at Payne again. "You with a crew or ridin' solo?"

When Payne didn't respond, the sheriff gave him a sideways glare. "Well?"

"You told me to shut the hell up."

"That I did, young fella, but now I'd like you to answer my question."

"Just me. On a road trip for a few months, exploring the West Coast from south to north."

"So you're a drifter," the sheriff stated.

"The very definition of that word is someone who wanders aimlessly, and I just indicated my travel plans."

"Said during the drive here that he used to work as a risk-management consultant," muttered Monroe. She gave Payne an almost apologetic glance for her boss's abrasiveness.

"What the heck kinda job is that?" asked Hanson, who was busy emptying the contents of a glass sugar dispenser into his coffee mug.

Payne stood up, moving to the bars. "I provided safety training for Fortune 500 companies with employees overseas in less than friendly environments. It was my job to teach them how to travel in urban settings, how to avoid scam artists, and stuff like that."

The sheriff walked closer, staring at Payne. "How to shoot someone up and then jam their body in a truck…what about 'stuff like that'?"

Payne felt like there were more than iron bars separating him from the man on the other side. "So, let me guess, in a small town like this, you must have a gavel that goes with that pistol."

Hanson stirred his coffee for an inordinate amount of time while glaring at Payne. "You sure are a smart-ass."

Monroe cleared her throat. "Mitch said he estimates the time of death to be sometime yesterday afternoon," she said referring to the forensics guy. "Payne says he was at Lassen Volcanic National Park most of yesterday until driving to the campsite in the evening. I'm going to call over to the park and see if they have any footage of him at the visitor center or the entrance booth."

Payne stood, moving closer to the bars. "My question is: why did someone want all of you to focus on me? Clearly, someone is trying to divert your attention. But why? Oh, and there's that other thing…there's still a killer on the loose."

Monroe and Hanson gave each other uneasy glances; even the secretary stopped typing for a moment as she looked at him. He figured they must have already been mulling over such things, but he wanted to drive those points home.

Unless Hanson or one of his deputies was behind the murder, in which case there will be a recently discharged 9mm pistol mysteriously discovered at my campsite.

He gazed at Monroe. Payne had encountered his share of killers and psychopaths over the years, and she didn't strike him as either. As for Hanson, he wasn't sure yet.

You don't get to be long in the tooth in his profession without collecting a shitload of enemies. Except, out in these parts, he would have dumped the body in some backcountry grave rather than on the side of the road.

Clearly, someone needed Payne as a fall guy, but who and why? Frankly, he didn't care. He just needed the deputies to complete their forensics and gunshot analysis and clear his name so he could get the hell out of California. But the felony possession of an unregistered firearm was going to complicate that.

Hanson motioned for his deputy to follow him, both of them heading down the hallway into one of the offices.

Payne returned to the bed, this time lying down as his mind sifted through the strange turn of events. He thought of the tattered metal sign on the edge of town.

"Absynth. Population 7,062. Welcome to our happy community."

Yeah, welcome to paradise.

CHAPTER 3

Eva Daly grabbed her checked luggage from the carousel at LAX and proceeded to the exit doors, making her way to the taxi driver at the curb.

After briefly conversing with him about her destination, Eva slid into the rear seat. She turned her attention to her phone, seeing her brother still hadn't responded to the half-dozen messages she'd left for him during the past twenty-four hours since receiving his cryptic text.

Her heart nearly punched through her chest when the phone rang. She clutched it tightly, staring at the number, only to be disappointed at seeing it was her editor from the *LA Times* calling.

"You get in alright?" asked Martin Buckley.

"Yeah, bumpy as hell after departing Bucharest, but the rest wasn't too bad."

"Tell me again why you wanted to visit Romania after the assignment in Turkey?"

"Transylvania. Prince Vlad. Dracula. Did you not hear anything I said when we talked last weekend?"

"Oh, yeah, your fascination with vampires and Goth

stuff?"

"Shut up. I never said anything about Goth."

"How long before you can get me the draft on the international summit in Turkey?"

"It's done. I'll send it over shortly."

"Damn, Eva, you're a machine."

"I wasn't about to waste nineteen hours on a flight watching movies and throwing down shots."

"Take a few days off. You've earned it. Then we need to talk about the Oslo trip next month. That trade delegation is going to be a whopper with a lot of big names from the tech world, and I want you there."

She sighed as much from the dread of being bottled up on another international flight as from the bumper-to-bumper traffic around the airport. "I'll get in touch early next week. And just a heads-up, I might be off-grid for a few days, so your calls will probably go straight to voicemail."

Martin chuckled. "Heading to some cabin in the sticks or something?"

"Pretty close. I can't get ahold of my brother up in Absynth, so a road trip might be in order, which means nine hours in my car."

"He's the bug guy, right?"

"Entomologist, genius. I thought you majored in English before you studied journalism?"

"I took *an* English class, then discovered there were more women in journalism."

"Your motivation for the profession was so pure," she said in a sarcasm-laced tone.

"What in God's name is your brother doing in Ass Crack, I mean Absynth, anyway?"

"We grew up there."

"I thought you were from Redding?"

"Most of my teens were spent in Redding, working for my

uncle's newspaper, but Aaron and I were born and raised in Absynth."

"Sorry to hear that. But you still turned out somewhat cultured, thankfully."

"Haha."

Her head was pounding from the jet lag, crowds, and elevation changes. And she had a gnawing feeling that something was amiss with her brother.

She brushed a strand of brunette hair off her left cheek, then massaged her temple. "Look, I'm almost at my apartment. I'll email you the article and be in touch next week."

"Take care and get some rest."

She slid the phone back in her jacket pocket, staring through the front window at the river of red brake lights on the highway. Eva kept her hand pressed against the phone, praying it would ring. And then Aaron would explain how he had been out in the field, immersed in research, and had let the hours slip away like he always did.

Except this time feels different.

She pulled out the device, retrieving the last text from her brother.

> It's like I was telling you all along. W is up to something beyond what anyone imagined. My research can prove it. Call me as soon as you get this.

Eva let her gaze wander out to the skyline, feeling like there was still an ocean of distance between her and Aaron.

She fondled the phone as if it were a life preserver keeping her afloat. Eva scrolled through her address book, located a number and called.

The monotone voice of Gabriel Joyce filled her ear. Joyce was the head of the insect pathology department with the California USDA and frequently employed Aaron for annual surveys. "Gabe, this is Eva Daly. I know it's been a long time, but do you have a minute?"

"Eva, God, it's good to hear from you. I was actually thinking about reaching out to you, but I don't have your number."

She felt a lump in her throat. "*You* were going to call me. Why? Is this about Aaron?"

"Yeah, have you heard from him lately? I left, like, a number of messages for him in the past day. He was doing some contract work for me, surveying sites north of Redding, and was supposed to call me this morning at the latest. You know him, I figured he was off-grid for the day, but now I'm wondering if he got stuck in the backcountry or something."

Eva felt nauseous, the words feeling like they were lodged in her throat as she spoke. "I, um, no, haven't talked to him since last week, but he left me a text yesterday morning. That's the last I've heard. What's going on?"

"That's what I'd like to know. He called me over the weekend, said he found something bizarre up by a meadow on the southwest side of Absynth during his annual insect survey. It was a lined bark beetle. He mailed me a preserved specimen to see if I could confirm his findings since I'm better equipped down here."

She scrunched her eyebrows together, trying to hold down her lunch as the Uber driver wove between cars on the highway. "An insect...what kind...and why would he be so concerned about that?"

"That's what I wondered, but he didn't go into great detail except to say it was an invasive never documented on the West Coast or even in this country. I got the specimen two days ago and confirmed it was *Cryptolestes pusillus,* which is supposed to be found only in Europe. And this particular insect had a rare fungus on its exoskeleton."

She rubbed her weary face with her other hand. "Let me guess, this beetle feeds on wheat."

A heavy sigh could be heard on the phone before Joyce responded, "So Aaron did fill you in on his hunch?"

"Not exactly. When we spoke a few weeks ago, he mentioned finding an unusual beetle in the fields near an agro-facility."

"Look, whatever is going on in Absynth, whatever your brother stumbled onto, is big. I mean really big. Finding multiple specimens of an insect with a potential fungal pathogen like this is not a random thing. Fortunately, the wheat in the US is a completely different strain with their own crop pests, so this beetle doesn't pose a threat to this region of the world."

She glanced at the exit ahead. "Hey, I'm headed home and then need to change and drop off my stuff. Can I swing over to your lab?"

"I'm actually at a field site east of Riverside until tomorrow afternoon. Let's shoot for then, say three o'clock. Remember that coffee shop on Pico Boulevard?"

"Jitters, yeah. I'll see you there. Thanks, Gabe."

———

THE TWO MEN in the black Suburban remained one vehicle behind the Uber driver's Toyota Prius.

Though the traffic congestion was considerable at this time of day, the Suburban driver, Jacob Schulz, still found it easier than trying to blend into the narrow streets in his home country of Bulgaria.

"Let the boss know what we're doing," he said to Simon Regal, the burly man with a thick black beard in the passenger's seat.

Regal made the call, putting his phone on speaker. Their superior on the other end answered on the first ring.

"She arrived a few minutes ago. Heading north, probably back to her apartment. What do you want us to do?" inquired Schulz.

"Observe for now," said Karl Wagner. "Elke bugged her place with audio earlier today, so we'll hear everything that's going on."

Schulz leaned in. "And if we hear anything actionable about her brother's research?"

"Call me immediately but don't make a move on her. We need her to lead us to it first."

"Just to confirm, the brother's permanently out of the picture, right?" asked Schulz.

"Yes, after he was caught snooping around the Wayland agro-site outside of Absynth, but she doesn't know that. And I need to find out where he stored his research files, or the millions of euros our employer sank into this operation could be blown to hell."

"So should we plan to drive north tomorrow?"

"Let's see what happens tonight and who she calls, but yes, we might all be heading to that rat-shit town very soon."

The driver and his passenger both shot each other surprised glances. "You're coming too?"

"The whole team. I want Daly's research and have no plan to search for days. We get in, get what we need and then eliminate Eva Daly."

"Forgive me for asking, sir, but we're all going to stand out in a small town."

Measured breathing on the phone ensued for a moment. "Except there won't be any witnesses left alive to ID us."

CHAPTER 4

Two hours later, Payne heard the front door of the sheriff's department open and saw Kessel and the bearded forensics analyst walk in.

Monroe emerged from the hallway, heading to the latter individual and speaking to him, but Payne couldn't make out their conversation. By the man's body posture, he was used to taking orders from her, and Payne wondered if Hanson actually ran the place or had put Monroe in charge, since Payne had earlier heard what sounded like snoring coming from a room down the hall.

After they finished conversing, the analyst headed to an office opposite the holding cell, returning a minute later with a swab kit. Monroe removed the keys from her belt and unlocked Payne's holding cell. She stood in the entrance, staring at him. "My forensics guy, Mitch, needs to do a gunpowder residue test on your hands and clothing. All you have to do is stand and remain still." She rested her hand on her Taser. "Is that going to be a problem, Mr. Payne?"

He got up, keeping his cuffed hands in front of his waist. "Nope, I'll just stare at you the whole time."

He wasn't being sarcastic, though he noted her frown. With her striking brown eyes, tan face and athletic figure, she was easy on the eyes and was, without a doubt, the nicest sight he'd seen in weeks.

Kessel had returned and stood outside the cell, scrutinizing Payne. From his slightly sagging shoulders, Kessel's earlier pistol-waving rage seemed to have dissipated; or his morning caffeine rush was ebbing; or maybe his partner had said something to deflate his ego so he didn't fly off the handle.

"He refuse a court-appointed lawyer?" asked Kessel.

She nodded.

"What about his gun...anything show up on the ATF database?"

"It's registered to someone in Pineland, Arizona. He said it belonged to a friend who died a few months back."

"More like he whacked the owner and took it for himself."

Payne fixed his gaze directly on the deputy. The man returned the look while folding his arms. Payne remained motionless, his face expressionless as he continued his piercing stare.

"Quite a tough guy, eh?" said Kessel, who eventually broke contact and turned, walking down the hallway.

Monroe stepped inside the small cell, standing in the corner as Mitch entered. "You know, you should think about easing up on the attitude," she said.

Payne canted his head. "I've been arrested for a murder I didn't commit and dragged away from my campsite, so this current attitude is about as toned down as I can muster."

————

Two hours later, Hanson and Monroe headed to the sheriff's office. She made sure the door was closed.

Monroe pulled up a chair across from his wooden desk. "Mitch said his initial analysis indicates that the vic was shot by three 9mm hollow-point rounds in the gut. Time of death was, as mentioned before, yesterday afternoon. All of that, and the fact that Mitch didn't find a single trace of gunshot residue on Mr. Payne, would seem to rule him out. I'm still waiting to hear back from Lassen National Park, though, about him being there yesterday."

Hanson rubbed an old scar on his forearm. "Put him in the tank downstairs for now. So far, he's the only suspect, though it sounds like he might not be much of one anymore. Did you check with Tommy Larkin about Payne being enrolled in his animal-tracking class at the field station?"

"Yeah, Tommy said he spoke with Payne on the phone a few weeks ago and that he was signed up for both days. Also said he seemed to know a lot about the subject and was mainly interested in picking Tommy's brain about his days working for the state as a cougar hunter during depredation cases."

She cleared her throat. "There's one other thing: Mitch said the vic's face was chewed up by what he thinks was a dog or maybe coyotes, which is why we weren't able to ID him. Plus, the plates on his vehicle were gone, and someone scratched out the VIN. Someone really wanted to bog down our investigation."

Monroe lowered her voice, hearing someone walk by. "It's taken a while, but the fingerprints indicate it's Aaron Daly."

Hanson leaned back, seething out an exhale. "Shit. Knew his folks. He was a good kid." He gazed at her. "You think this could be connected with those other victims from this past spring and summer? What people around here are calling 'the Ghost Murders'?"

She shook her head. "Not sure what the connection would be since those bodies were all found in remote side canyons, and all suffered single gunshot wounds. Long-distance rifle rounds to the head, not gutshots from a pistol at close range."

"Yeah, I suppose. Was just wondering since you worked those cases more than me." He stood, pacing for a moment. "We should have Dottie see about locating Aaron's sister, Eva. She's the only one left now from that dynasty."

"Dynasty, seriously? They weren't royalty."

"They were one of the founding families of this town. Hell, half the properties around here used to belong to them when I was a kid, and her grandfather owned that newspaper in Redding, so their turf extended quite a ways."

He paused, turning towards her. "In fact, once you locate her, you should look into Eva's whereabouts yesterday."

"What…you think she murdered her own brother?" Monroe shook her head. "Look, I knew both of them. Eva and I were in the same classes together in high school. She may have acted like she was better than the rest of us, but she's no killer."

"High school was a ways off. People change. You stay in this business long enough, Becky, and you'll start to witness things you could never imagine. I'm always amazed at how money and power can warp a human being, like one of those twisted tree roots you see along the edge of a canyon."

He gave her a hard stare. "And now Eva is suddenly the sole inheritor of the Daly fortune."

————

AFTER PAYNE'S processing was completed, he was escorted downstairs by Monroe and Kessel to a large holding cell containing six other individuals.

The lower level was spacious, and Payne figured the thirty-by-thirty prisoner-containment area was used for the entire county, given Absynth was the largest town in the region.

Kessel stopped at the wrought-iron entrance gate on the right, removing the key off his belt and opening the lock.

"How long am I going to be down here?" he asked, turning to address Monroe.

"Until the van from Redding comes to transfer you down-state to the big house," said Kessel, motioning for Payne to step inside the cell.

"Depends on if your alibi checks out and if my forensics team finds anything of significance," said Monroe, who closed the gate and had him place his hands through the bars to unlock his cuffs.

"And how long will all of that take?"

She sighed, withdrawing the cuffs and nodding at the other prisoners. "Just sit tight; there's a line ahead of you."

Kessel walked to the end of the walkway and sat down on a chair in the corner, grabbing a hunting magazine off the table beside it. "I'll take babysitting duty until noon."

"I'll come back as soon as I get the other cases sorted out," she said, turning and walking towards the staircase.

Payne pivoted around, studying his new cage. But it wasn't the setting as much as the sight of Merle and two of his men in the corner that made his pulse quicken.

CHAPTER 5

THE AROMA OF CEDAR TREES WAFTED THROUGH THE OPEN window beside Matt Graves' home office. He looked past the faded white curtains and up at the sky, seeing a low row of cumulus clouds beginning to stack up around Pittman Mountain in the distance.

Coupled with the morning weather report, he knew the clouds were precursors of a large Pacific storm that would blanket the region soon. While he normally welcomed such precipitation, this amount of rain was sure to wreak havoc on his cannabis operations, which were spread around the remote valley floor.

With only a couple of weeks until harvest, Graves, or McG as he was known to his crew, worried that the numerous ATV roads leading to his scattered pot fields would be washed away, which would result in diverting his workforce from perimeter security to road maintenance so the crops could be accessed in time.

He heard the familiar footsteps of his uncle as the older man climbed up the creaky wooden steps to the second floor of the house. Amos Graves walked with a cane, ambling towards a recliner in the corner and plunking down like he'd just ascended a mountain summit.

"Just got word from one of our contacts in Absynth that your guy Merle and two of his crew were processed into the sheriff's department for sexually harassing a couple of women in town."

Graves leaned back, stroking his black goatee. "Fuck, you've got to be kidding."

"I told you that hiring that meth-head and his freaks would come back to bite us."

"He knows to keep his mouth shut. Plus, he's been a reliable distributor for the past six months, and I need his contacts in Riverside. They've got a direct pipeline to Phoenix and Albuquerque that's bringing in a decent cash flow."

Amos interlaced his thick fingers across his belly. "It's your show now. I'm too old to be making the decisions on who is hired and how our product gets circulated, but you should really think about cutting Merle loose after this season. He's too unpredictable and has a history of violence that could draw attention back to us."

Graves sighed, staring up at the clouds again. Since taking over the cannabis business from his uncle three years ago after the old man suffered a mild stroke, Graves had been under considerable pressure to keep the family enterprise in the black. If it wasn't the weather impacting his bottom line, then it was the constant monthly road trips to his out-of-state buyers in New York and the East Coast, along with competition from fledgling growers moving into northern California.

Graves had recently seen to the latter threat by purchasing available land in the region to expand his empire. And with the cash inflow from a new alliance with the Wayland Corporation, he would be able to purchase the remaining parcels in the valley.

Amos and his wife, Olivia, had settled in this remote area

in the late '70s after the plethora of hippy communes folded, buying up a forty-acre vegetable farm twelve miles down a dead-end dirt road that they slowly converted into a small cannabis plantation.

After Graves suffered the loss of his parents in a car accident during freshman year in high school in LA, he was taken in by Amos and introduced to the underground economy of the cannabis world. Eventually, Graves brought his technological acumen into the business through the use of drones, motion cameras and an encrypted comms system to keep in touch with his workers at the scattered off-grid farms. And having a Filipino father, Graves used his former connections to that culture in LA to recruit some of his labor force.

Now, all McG needed was to have a successful harvest in late October and finish out his agreement to provide external security for the Wayland agro-facility. This would provide him with the much-needed funds to buy up the last two hundred acres of private property on the other side of the mountain, ensuring his dominion over the region.

His iPhone rang, and he felt a pang of anxiety when he saw the number.

"This is McG."

"The coroner should have completed his findings by now on Daly. I just want to make sure nothing is traced back here," said Anton Fischer, the head of security for the Wayland agro-site fifteen miles south of Graves' place.

"I said before that you don't have to worry. My guys took care of it and pinned it on a drifter staying at one of the nearby campgrounds."

"Hanson and his stooges bought the story?"

"Last I heard from my contact in town, they're holding the guy and have all their manpower focused on him, so we're in the clear for a while. Once the sheriff starts piecing things together, our business partnership will be nearing completion, so there won't be anything left to trace at all."

"I don't need to remind you that these next few days are critical. Our research is nearly done, and we'll be packing up by early next week, if not sooner, depending on this fucking weather."

"What do you need from me?" Graves hoped nothing, since he already had a small crew of his guys staked out around the Wayland site and needed all his manpower focused on his own plantation sites.

"I've just received word that some of my superiors may be coming from downstate. If that happens, then they may require your help since you know the lay of the land better than myself."

"Help for what?"

"I'll keep you posted. Just stay in range. I don't want to hear any excuses about being off-grid. Carry your satellite phone at all times. If this goes down, then it'll be in the next day or two."

Graves tossed the phone on his desk. He wasn't used to taking orders from anyone and wanted nothing more than to throat punch Fischer.

"More problems?" said his uncle.

"I'll just be glad when the gig with those maggots at Wayland is over."

"I remember when they first took over that old property and retrofitted the place with all their research labs. Back then, they were just a commercial ag-site, doing studies on barley and wheat crops." He raised his hands. "But this past year, it sure seems like they've gotten into some other shit that makes me scratch my head, especially since it seemed important enough to silence that Daly kid."

Graves swiveled in his seat, staring at his barn across the field, where his guys were offloading fertilizer from a trailer.

"All I know is that their soil scientist's recommendations on where to plant this year's harvest around the mountain made a huge difference."

"Yeah, I thought I knew it all but was surprised at the results." He waved his cane at Graves. "Just remember, there's always someone cleverer than yourself."

Graves gave his uncle a perfunctory nod, knowing that being clever was only a small piece of the pie, and that ruthlessness and brutality played a far greater role.

CHAPTER 6

THE LARGE HOLDING CELL WAS SPACIOUS COMPARED TO THE upstairs accommodations, with steel benches bolted to the floor that extended around the perimeter of the place. Given the raw odor of beer and urine, Payne was sure the stench had saturated every pore in the concrete floor, and the slow movement of the ceiling fan did little to dissipate the odor.

Six inmates were spread around the room. The only two women were huddled near each other and looked like they had spent the night sleeping in a muddy ditch, given their ruddy faces and unkempt hair. To the right of them was a thirty-something man who was frantically scratching his forearm and muttering religious epithets, like he was trying to cast out a demon from under his skin.

But it was the other three occupants that made Payne feel like he had just entered a den of vipers. Seated in the left corner was the goon with a penchant for beer-laced popcorn.

Merle, was it?

The man noticed the new arrival, his eyes locking onto Payne as he whispered something to the two burly men sitting beside him.

Payne walked to the empty corner on the right, plunking down on the tarnished bench and pressing his back against the steel bars.

The loner near the two women canted his head towards Payne, speaking in a low whisper as his blue eyes emitted a wild look. "They get their paws on you too?"

"Who?"

"Hold up your hands for a second, man."

Payne flared an eyebrow, indulging the guy, who then scrutinized his hands.

"Yeah, that's what I thought...you got good working hands for digging in the mines like me. But it looks like you got away. Not for long, though. They'll find us. No prison's gonna keep 'em out."

"What the hell are you talking about?"

"The Sasquatch that live in the foothills. They grab people all the time, man, and make 'em dig in the diamond mines up in the mountains. Then, when 'Squatch get enough diamonds, they signal the aliens who come to refuel their ships with the precious stones, that's why there's so many missing hikers in these parts. It's the aliens in league with the 'Squatch. They've been doing it for thousands of years."

The guy leaned in, his stale breath causing Payne to slide back. "Or it could be the Ghost that's getting 'em. Some say he's a vengeful spirit that snatches up the souls of the evil who wander into the woods. He's new in these parts, though, unlike the 'Squatch. Of course, maybe they're all working together."

"It's a good thing I won't be around here for long, then." Payne slid farther into the corner, wishing he could get back the last five minutes of his life and wondering if there was LSD in the town's water supply.

He watched Kessel grab the empty coffee pitcher on the table and head up the stairs.

Payne extended his legs and folded his arms while leaning his head back, lowering his eyelids slightly, but not enough to obscure keeping tabs on the three thugs in the opposite corner. His brief respite didn't last long.

"Hey, pigeon-lover, you're not acting so tough now, are you?"

Payne didn't have to gaze at the goon with the greasy black hair to know who was talking. He'd wondered how long it would be before the man named Merle would feel the need to brandish the newfound courage that came with the company of his two hulking compatriots.

Merle spit on the floor. "Hey, bird-boy. I'm talkin' to your sorry ass."

Payne sighed. He glanced at the two security cameras on the walls beyond the cell, knowing anything he said or did would be recorded.

"Is there a question in there?" asked Payne, feigning indifference by closing his eyes momentarily.

"Yeah. I wanna know why your punk ass is up in my neck of the woods?"

"That means you must be with the welcoming committee from the Chamber of Commerce," said Payne. "Maybe you can tell me if there's a fall festival coming up soon. I could sure go for some apple cider and cinnamon donuts."

"Answer the fuckin' question," said the surly bruiser on the right, whose oaken arms were peppered with crude tattoos.

"Look, fellas, I'm in my corner, minding my own business, and don't want any trouble." He said it loud enough for the cameras.

"Fuck what you want," said the popcorn enthusiast. "You're on my turf now, and I make the rules."

"The fact that you're on this side of the bars says otherwise, actually."

Merle stood up, ambling across the center of the floor while his two buddies shadowed him. The thug on the right was a foot taller than his pals and wore a black leather vest, which accentuated his sunburned arms. His pockmarked cheeks made Payne wonder if his face had once caught fire and been put out with a bag of nickels.

The man on the left had a twisted nose and was someone who could have been a linebacker. By their size and caveman looks, Payne wondered if they had interbred with the Sasquatch.

Payne retracted his legs and sat upright, resting his hands on his knees.

Merle stopped a few feet away, while the larger men pressed in closer to their friend. By the way they angled their bodies, Payne figured it was to block the cameras.

He was wondering if the entrance door upstairs would buzz open with Kessel's return. Or if Sheriff Hanson was the kind of guy who had his boots up on his desk, about to enjoy the coming altercation.

Either way, Payne had to end this before a blow came crashing down on his head. And he had to drop the guy in the vest first, then his gargantuan friend. The determination being made by the sheer amount of scars on the hands of the man.

"You're not so shit hot in here like you was at that gas station." The squawker stepped forward to jab his finger at Payne's face.

Payne bolted upright, grabbing Merle's finger and snapping it back until it cracked, then shoving him into the tattooed goon on the right. Immediately, Payne dropped slightly and sent a vicious right cross into the other thug's groin. The man's legs buckled, and Payne followed with an uppercut with all of his weight packed into the strike. It connected with the lower jaw, and Payne was sure he heard some teeth crack.

Payne spun to his right, seeing a haymaker heading towards his head. He shot up both arms in a double forearm block, then slammed a hammer fist into his attacker's neck before stomping his boot down onto the man's instep, smashing the guy's bones. He followed that with a left hook, which connected with the man's cheek and drove him to the ground. Payne rushed back towards the other thug, who was staggering to his feet, and sent his knee into the guy's face.

His attention diverted back to Merle, who was clutching his broken finger and backpedaling towards the benches. "Easy, man. I was just messin' with you."

The entrance door to the hallway clicked open, and Monroe and Kessel rushed in, approaching the main gate.

"Did you see what this fucking animal did to us?" shouted Merle as he returned to help his two friends up. "We was just talking, and he starts all this kung fu shit."

"Shut up, Merle," said Monroe, who stood poised with her Taser. "All three of you get back to where you were sitting before."

She sent Payne a scrutinizing glance before reholstering her weapon.

"Those guys came at me," he said.

Monroe narrowed her eyes. "And you can be quiet, too." She glanced around the cell. "In fact, all of you just shut your pieholes and leave each other alone unless you want your stay here to drag past this weekend."

She turned towards Kessel. "Go get three ice packs. And then stay down here so you can watch these idiots."

Payne sat and leaned back into the steel bars again. This time, he closed his eyes, eagerly awaiting the time when he could ride the hell away from this backwater town.

CHAPTER 7
WAYLAND CORPORATE HQ, LOS ANGELES

THEO DAVENPORT SLID BACK FROM HIS LAPTOP AFTER REVIEWING the data from the chief entomologist at his Absynth agricultural facility. "Everything is on track. The weaponized pathogen is nearly complete, and the shipment will be ready for pickup this Sunday at the earliest."

Mikal Bana remained motionless, his granite face not revealing either pleasure or dissatisfaction.

But Davenport knew there would be no reason for the latter. After all, they were soon going to be wealthier than God.

He sat up, moving past his bodyguard and removing a solid block of clear polyurethane from his bookcase. He smiled, handing it to Bana.

The German oligarch examined the perfectly preserved insect inside. "This is what we are staking everything on? How many?"

"Millions once the initial batch is spread and starts to multiply."

Bana thrust it back at Davenport. "What guarantees can you provide that this will work as you say?"

"As we discussed before many times, my facility up north has been perfecting this insect strain, and all of the data from the past month indicates it will have a ninety-seven percent success rate for what we need."

Bana ran a hand through his thick black hair. "It is still a sizable risk on my end if this doesn't work and is traced back to me and my distribution network throughout Europe."

The Wayland CEO fixed his gaze on Bana. "While you are indeed providing your distribution channels overseas for dispersing the pathogen, so far, the risk in this venture has all been mine. We are using *my* agricultural research facility near Absynth, *my* research team developed the hybridized beetle, and *my* personnel removed Aaron Daly from the picture, not to mention how many other civilians will be added to that tally. If Daly's research sees the light of day, then this entire business venture is fucked." He waved his hand in the air. "Again, I am taking all the risk to line both of our pockets."

The German businessman drummed his fingers on the side of the leather chair. "You're right. A show of faith is in order." He motioned towards the lone figure standing silently near the door. "My man Karl has been monitoring Aaron Daly's sister since she arrived back in the US, as you requested. His team is tracking her right now and should soon know the location of the brother's data."

Bana motioned for Karl to step closer. "See to it personally that things go smoothly in Absynth. Nothing must interfere with the delivery of the product."

––––––––

WAGNER HAD STOOD QUIETLY WATCHING the business exchange unfold between his boss, Mikal Bana, and Theo Davenport. While he knew of Davenport's impressive résumé and background as a corporate mogul, he wondered about the extent of what Davenport knew about Bana's history beyond that of being an oligarch.

There was probably little on record about Bana's origins as a former German GSG operator turned mercenary who later became the head bodyguard to one of the most powerful crime families in Romania twenty years ago. And even less about how Bana eventually wed the man's daughter and, with her help, brutally killed her father and the other family members before taking the reins of the organization, which had its tentacles in every facet of the black market in Eastern Europe.

Bana only employed other former GSG operators like Wagner to keep his circle of loyalists tight and help prevent the inbred rivalries that he had witnessed within his wife's family. And Wagner was pleased that he and his team were finally allowed to go off-leash on American soil.

He found it amusing to observe Davenport trying to throw his weight around by citing his business accomplishments and acumen, unaware that he was sitting across from an alpha wolf who could eviscerate him in seconds, and who had his own methods for cornering his competitors.

Wagner wondered if he would one day be sent to eliminate Davenport after this current deal had gone through. He gazed at the American bodyguard near the CEO's desk, who resembled a gorilla stuffed into a suit. He knew the man had briefly been in the Marines and had attended a high-priced executive-protection school before this current job.

But Wagner felt a sense of ease knowing that the only people in this room with the blood of hundreds of men on their hands were on this side of the office.

CHAPTER 8

It was just after 4 p.m. when Deputy Monroe stepped through the security entrance and entered the hallway outside the holding cell. "Payne, you're up. Let's go."

He stood, walking to the lone gate. In the opposite corner of the hallway, Deputy Kessel barely glanced up from his *Sports Afield* magazine, but long enough to give a disapproving look.

"What now?" asked Payne.

She worked the key in the lock. "Your alibi checked out. Lassen National Park's security cams have you entering the building yesterday morning, and the entrance booth shows you leaving the park on your motorcycle at 3 p.m. And the gunpowder residue swab came up negative, though we'll be hanging on to your .38 revolver for the time being. You're in the clear, for now, anyway. The sheriff still wants you to stay within county limits."

He was puzzled why there was no mention of the felony offense of possessing the Smith & Wesson, but he wasn't willing to argue the point with someone holding the key to his release. "So I'm free, but not free. Why does he need me to stick around, exactly?"

"Because of the fact that someone clearly identified you as the individual connected with the murder, and your proximity to the crime scene. There's something odd going on, and until we know more, he wants you to stay close by."

She opened the cell as Kessel kept an eye on the other detainees. When she finished locking the gate, she motioned towards the stairs and followed Payne up.

Once on the main level, they passed by the other offices, stopping beside an open door on the right, which had her name listed on the smoky glass window.

"Wait here a second." Monroe stepped inside, sorting through a stack of papers on her desk.

The room was sparse with only a few framed certificates on the wall and a small bookcase with dusty shelves. Tilted at an angle towards her chair was a photo of two small boys with Monroe nestled between them. Earlier, he'd noticed the absence of a wedding band on her finger and now wondered if she was a single mother.

He took a step into the room, glancing at a framed photo on the wall that answered his question. This one looked like it had been dusted recently, the clear glass revealing an image of a decorated army soldier with a Ranger tab on his sleeve. Below the photograph was a personalized memorial plaque with the words Derek Monroe, Son, Father and Beloved Husband.

From the look of the soldier, he bore a family resemblance to the deputy.

So not her husband.

Regardless, Payne felt a pang of sadness for the deputy, thinking back to the friends and colleagues he'd lost over the years. Men and women who were among the living one minute, then spilling their blood on a mission in some part of the world that rarely made the headlines, their families never truly knowing the cause of their death while being told that their sacrifice was for the greater good.

Monroe turned around with a handful of papers. She gave him a surprised look that was laced with sorrow when she noticed what he was staring at. "I asked you to remain in the hallway."

He nodded. "My apologies. I was just curious."

She shot him a fierce gaze, thrusting her chin towards the entrance. "Let's head up front. I need you to sign a few things to process you out; then I'll get your personal items returned, minus your revolver. After that, I'll give you a lift back to the campground, since I need to check on the crime scene anyway."

He wasn't expecting the ride, but grateful he wouldn't have to pay for an Uber fare, which would be pricey in these parts.

However, he had no plans to stick around. Once back at the campground, he would pack up his site and head north into Oregon. He had no desire to stay for the upcoming tracking class with Larkin, wanting to get away from this grimy town and its strange underbelly.

Hopefully, he wouldn't encounter any Sasquatch during his exodus.

CHAPTER 9

AFTER MERLE DADE AND HIS TWO ASSOCIATES WERE RELEASED on bail a few hours before Payne, the men walked to the vehicle impoundment lot and retrieved their Chevy van.

Quinton, the burly man with the arm tattoos, drove them a half mile down Highway 3 to a convenience store and parked in a dirt lot at the rear of the building, pulling up beside a blue Ford Taurus with a cracked windshield and four men inside.

A tall man with a gray and black bowler hat emerged from the Taurus while Merle and Rodney stepped out of the van. Quinton remained inside the van with the engine running and his eyes trained on his surroundings.

"I drove up from Redding right after you called this morning, boss. I figured you guys woulda been here an hour ago, since I posted bail around eleven," said Angel Rodrigo, a gold crucifix around his neck glinting in the sun. He handed Merle a small Ziploc containing a handful of blue pills.

Merle grabbed it, removing two and popping the amphetamines into his mouth, then dry swallowing before passing the drugs to Rodney.

"Yeah, well, you know how things go in this shit-rag town," said Merle.

Rodrigo glanced down at the popsicle stick held in place with white tape around Merle's right index finger, then up at Rodney's bruised cheek. "What the hell happened?"

Merle just shook his head. "There's an outsider who's on my wanted list."

Merle pulled out his phone and looked up a location on Google Maps. When he was done, he leaned against the van, glancing at the road headed west into the mountains. With each passing moment, his grip on the phone intensified. He shifted his gaze to the other strung-out men inside the Taurus, then over to Rodrigo. "You got all our usual hardware in the trunk of your car?"

"As always. Enough firepower to tackle a small army."

"Good, I overheard the sheriff talking in his office when we were being processed out, about how that woman deputy was gonna give Payne a ride back to a campground west of here, since he was due for discharge soon. There's only one campground open in the area, and it's not too far west of here. I think we should check it out. If Payne is staying there, then we oughta give him a nice welcome."

Rodney gave Merle a nervous glance. "You sure about that, boss? We don't need any more run-ins with the law. Plus, you told McG we'd be picking up a shipment later tonight."

"So we wait until after Payne gets dropped off and is all alone. This time of year, campgrounds up north empty out, so no one will be around to hear his screams when I hack him to pieces."

CHAPTER 10

GABRIEL JOYCE PLUNKED HIS LAPTOP BAG DOWN ON THE COUCH in his two-story LA townhome and headed straight for the liquor cabinet above the fridge.

He pulled out a bottle of Johnny Walker and poured himself a glass. The ice cubes could wait. Joyce simply wanted to forget about his job at the USDA.

As if he didn't have enough to worry about with the upcoming fall report due with his boss in DC, his number one leading cereal-crop entomologist, Aaron Daly, had gone missing after discovering the impossible.

What the hell is Cryptolestes pusillus *doing in Absynth, California, of all places? What's that beetle even doing in North America for that matter? It can't physically exist here without its food source.*

He took a swig of the whiskey, which felt like a hot coal sliding down his throat. Immediately, his eyes widened, and he felt the rush of bile gurgling up from his stomach as he stared at someone standing in the corner near the patio door.

What the fuck? Joyce blinked hard, figuring the man in black must have entered through the second-floor balcony.

Joyce slid back, setting the liquor down and reaching for a kitchen knife attached to the magnetic fixture on the wall. His actions seemed futile as the man raised a suppressed pistol, leveling it at Joyce's chest.

"All the money I have is in my dresser. Just take it and go."

The man emitted a faint smile. "Do I look like I'm here to rob you, Gabe?"

Joyce backed up until he was pressed against the pantry closet. "Do I know you?"

"I am of little consequence. However, your texts and messages with Aaron Daly are of great consequence to me."

"Aaron…what's Aaron got to do with anything?"

"The insect samples he collected near Absynth, where are they?"

Joyce licked his dry lips. "The insect specimen was at my lab, but it was destroyed since it's an invasive and I completed my analysis. The report is on my laptop on the couch."

The man remained motionless, his dark brown eyes scrutinizing Joyce. It was a look the researcher had observed amongst lions on an African safari last year.

"Who else knows about Daly's findings in Absynth besides you and his sister, Eva?"

Joyce felt his ribs constrict and bile rush further into his throat. "Oh, God, please don't do anything to Eva. She doesn't know anything."

He stepped closer. "Who else knows?"

Joyce shook his head, his knees buckling. "No one."

The man squeezed the pistol's trigger, splintering apart Joyce's skull and spraying pink mist onto the pantry door.

KARL WAGNER REMOVED the suppressor from his 9mm HK pistol and placed the pistol back in its concealment holster under his shirt. He headed to the couch, sifting through Joyce's laptop bag. He'd already searched the rest of the townhome, gathering a tablet, notebooks and a dozen flash drives.

He returned to the kitchen, rifling through Joyce's pockets and removing his phone and car keys. He would have to do a search of the dead man's vehicle, but that should wrap up his work here.

His own phone rang, and he pulled the device from his jacket pocket. "What do you have for me?"

Wagner's second-in-command, Jacob Schulz, replied, "Eva Daly wasn't home for long. From the audio, it seemed like she was spooked, thinking someone had been in her place since she found something moved on her dresser. One of our team must have been sloppy."

"Cops get involved?"

"No. She called a friend. A woman named Bethany. Eva is driving over to her apartment to spend the night. We're following her as we speak."

"Good, get me an address and I'll head over there."

"There's one other problem: I looked up this woman Bethany; she's a fucking reporter for the LA Times, just like Eva."

Wagner balled a fist. "Once you're at the apartment complex, find a way to set up eavesdropping equipment. I need ears on their conversation. Maybe Eva will mention more about her conversations with her brother."

"Or we could just grab both women and use Bethany to leverage Daly into talking."

"Normally, I'd agree, but the messages between Eva and her brother the Wayland guys discovered on Aaron's phone were pretty sketchy. She may not even know where he kept his research findings. If that's the case, then her next move will probably be heading to Absynth."

"And what about this woman Bethany?"

Wagner glanced down at the dead man's slumped figure. "I think the coroner's office will be putting in some overtime this week."

CHAPTER 11

PAYNE SAT IN THE REAR OF THE POLICE VEHICLE, THIS TIME riding in Monroe's Ford Bronco with the Absynth County logo. The thirty-minute drive to the campground was punctuated with Monroe serving as a local tour guide by pointing out the prominent waterfalls, hiking trails and historical monuments along the way.

He remained silent, disinterested in any of the natural or cultural features of the region, while counting the minutes until he was straddling his motorcycle and on his way north away from this region. He also hoped to avoid any further run-ins with Merle and his miscreants, though he figured the guy was probably passed out in a cheap motel in Redding by now.

As if reading his thoughts, she glanced at him in the rearview mirror. "I know you're pissed off, and you have every right to be. I would be, too, but please don't get any ideas about heading out of the county." Her voice had softened from the flat tone of the cop.

"Sure." He glanced out the right window at a dirt road

with a sign indicating it led to the trailhead for Beachum Gulch.

"You probably didn't get to see much of it, but Absynth has a really nice historic district downtown with some great restaurants and even a museum devoted to the Prohibition. This was the epicenter of a large rum-running ring back in the day."

"You also work for the Chamber of Commerce?"

She frowned. "Look, Mr. Payne, I regret that your introduction to our little community went the way it did and hope you'll give it another chance, especially since you're sticking around for that field course with Larkin."

He couldn't figure out her angle. Was she just playing nice to make sure he stayed in the county during the investigation so she didn't have more work tracking him down? *And how come there were no charges being pressed for firearms possession?*

"Call me Kyle. 'Mr. Payne' makes me feel much older than I am."

"Thirty-eight, right?" She shot a quick glance in the mirror again.

He nodded, rubbing an old elbow injury that made him feel a decade older. "And you? I'd say thirty, maybe." He suspected it was five years more, but no need to push his luck with a woman who was being his personal taxi driver.

She canted her head. "You know, most women would not take kindly to fielding that question, especially from a stranger."

"Considering you know quite a lot about me already, 'stranger' doesn't seem like an appropriate moniker."

"What I'd like to know is how you bowled through those three morons back at the jail like they were toy soldiers. I rewatched the video footage, and you set those guys up and picked them apart like you'd done that sorta thing more than a few times."

"Grew up in a rough neighborhood, and the walk to school was fraught with punks like those guys."

She shook her head. "Nice try, except I looked up Ishpeming, Michigan, and it's surrounded by miles of forests and swamp and has a population of fifty-four hundred. The only thing you were battling on the walk to school were mosquitos."

"Bravo. You've done your homework, as I'd expect from a professional like yourself. Except you overlooked the fact that those mosquitos were the size of ravens and worked in packs, hunting down kids. I lost at least one friend a week to those vicious beasts."

She came to a four-way stop, pausing, then proceeding straight. "I can't tell if you're normally sarcastic or just trying to deflect my questions?"

"It's a fine blend, actually. I've been working on my stagecraft for a few years in case I ever had a deputy for a chauffeur."

Monroe thrust her chin at the green sign for the campground. "Well, I just hope you tip as well as you bullshit; then the ride will have been worth it."

A few moments of silence ensued before she spoke again. "How do you sleep in a hammock? That seems like it would be pretty uncomfortable. Why not use a tent?"

"Just something I got used to, I guess. Grew up with a dad who's a game warden, and I spent a lot of time in the wilds. When I was older, he used to take me on some of his investigations, which meant we'd be camped out in the backcountry for a few days. Hammocks worked well because we could hop up quickly and be on our feet compared with being trapped inside a tent."

"What was he investigating?"

"Illegal hunting and poaching, mostly."

"What's the difference?"

"Quite a few guys would go hunting deer or wild turkey out of season, mostly for the meat. Poachers would kill for the trophy, because they're boys in men's bodies who need the ego boost of having a mighty head mounted on their wall at home. And then, of course, there are bear poachers after the gallbladders, which are shipped in coolers back to Asia for medicinal uses."

"You must be close with your dad after spending so much time like that with him." She gazed out her window. "Mine seemed like he was gone most of my childhood. Long-distance truck driver...the highway was his home much of the year. My brother and I spent more time at my neighbor's place. He and his wife are the ones who practically raised us."

Monroe glanced at him again in the mirror, holding her eyes on him a little longer. "He was my kid brother, by the way. The photo on the wall in my office."

Payne pursed his lips. "I'm sorry for your loss."

There was a pregnant silence for a long while. "Hardest part is the not knowing. Derek died a year ago this week, killed who knows where. It's the 'where' part that tears me apart, wondering what he was doing during his final moments on this Earth."

"So were those his kids in the photo on the bookcase?"

She nodded. "My nephews live with my sister-in-law, but we're all close, and I look out for them. I always will."

"I saw the Ranger tab. Those are some tough fellas."

"He was, for sure, but his service had worn him out on so many levels. Too many deployments and too much horror in places he could never talk about."

Payne carefully thought through his response, not wanting to tip her off to his background in clandestine services. "Being in the risk-management field overseas, I've had a few friends in the spec-ops community who were involved in things the American public would never get behind. That life of secrecy, and the carnage that goes with it, eventually takes a toll on more than just the body."

Hell, that's why I'm a full-time vagabond now.

Her eyes momentarily teared, and she turned away from the rearview mirror. "Derek was also a helluva practical joker. And a smart-ass, like you."

"Is that why you've cut me slack since you arrested me? No offense, but you almost seemed like you were just going through the motions at the campground this morning, as if you were bored."

"The whole thing was odd from the get-go, starting with the anonymous call to the sheriff and then your deer-in-the-headlights expression when we showed up. You didn't strike me as someone who had just been busted for murder. I was thinking along the lines of what you said earlier: why would you kill someone, leave their vehicle visible on the road nearby, and then return to the campsite for breakfast?"

"Thank you for making me not sound crazy."

She glanced at him in the mirror again. "Plus, I have a good feel for people, and you don't seem like a killer. A brawler, maybe, but not a killer."

Payne wondered how someone in law enforcement could be such a terrible judge of character.

––––––

PAYNE EAGERLY AWAITED the last mile to the campground turnoff as they drove past the stretch of road where the dead man had been found and from which Payne's troubles had sprung.

He recalled the mortified expression on Monroe's face when looking at the corpse. "You seemed to have a look of recognition at the crime scene...has that kind of thing happened in these parts before?"

"Yeah, but not recently. And it's mostly stolen vehicles out of Weaverville that get dumped near the outskirts of town, not gunshot victims."

"I imagine a grisly murder in these parts must send a shock wave through the community. I know it would in my small hometown."

"It hasn't been broadcast yet, so please don't mention it to anyone."

"I'll try to keep away from the overbearing crowds at the campground, so no worries." He glanced back up at his driver. "I hope you eventually get some answers about your brother so you can have some closure. It's hard living with so many unanswered questions swimming in your head."

"Thanks. I appreciate that. I'm not sure why I told you. I rarely speak about it. Maybe you do remind me of him a little." She turned down the loop leading to his campsite.

Unlike her two colleagues, she had a quiet confidence and amiability that made her easy to talk with, not to mention being a great-looking woman.

"Deputy Monroe, I thank you for the ride." He felt like saying more and wondered what might have unfolded if they had met under different circumstances.

Monroe was quiet, gazing at him briefly again in the mirror. She came to a halt by his campsite.

Payne stepped out, relieved to see his Indian motorcycle standing dormant beside the picnic table and his hammock camping setup in the distance.

He leaned in on the open window of the passenger's side. "Good luck with your manhunt."

"Who says it's a man?"

She was right. He'd known more than his share of lethal, cold-blooded killers of the opposite sex, but they were the exception. "Statistics."

"You gonna be able to relax out here, knowing there's

someone still running around? Maybe you should grab a place in town."

He nodded, figuring he'd be across the Oregon state line by nightfall and would find another campsite in the woods. "I'll be alright. Take care of yourself, Deputy."

She waved, then put the Bronco in gear and slowly drove off.

He walked to the picnic table, picking up the tipped-over bowl that had contained his oatmeal, along with the other items that had blown onto the ground.

Once he saw the Bronco disappear completely, he went about quickly packing up the campsite, stuffing the gear into the side panniers on the motorcycle.

But it was a familiar acrid odor from the jail, which floated across on the breeze, that made him realize he wasn't alone.

CHAPTER 12

MONROE WOVE THE BRONCO THROUGH THE LAST OF THE FIGURE-
eight loops of campsites and drove back towards the main
entrance. Pausing beside the self-pay station on the gravel
shoulder, she glanced down a narrow dirt road on the right,
where a twelve-foot section of rusted chain was lying on the
ground.

She hadn't noticed it earlier upon arrival, but the chain
was normally suspended between two yellow concrete posts,
banning entrance to the pump house, which provided well
water for the campground.

Monroe exited the Bronco and walked over to the downed
barrier. The padlock had been cut, and there were fresh
vehicle tracks heading down the road. The sight of a familiar
white van from the impoundment lot sent an icy chill down
her spine.

And the gunshots ringing out in the woods behind her
told her Merle and his goons had come for payback.

———

DETECTING the foul body odor of his attackers didn't help prevent the coming rush as a machete-wielding man bolted out from behind a tall boulder a few feet from Payne's hammock. It was the burly man with the tattooed arms from the jail, only he had a deranged look in his bloodshot eyes, like he was amped on something.

Payne barely sidestepped in time to prevent the tip of the blade from shearing off his nose. The machete sliced into the pine tree to the left. With the killer struggling to free his weapon, Payne lunged forward, driving a palm strike into the man's jaw and sending him back into the boulder, his head cracking on the rock.

Payne felt something slam into his back, the shock wave compressing his ribs and causing his knees to buckle. He collapsed to one knee, going with the momentum and rolling off to his left side as the baseball bat connected with the boulder. Payne saw a wild-eyed man with a goatee arching up for another strike, and he shot a kick into the thug's groin. With his attacker's momentum deflated, Payne grabbed a palm-sized rock and flung it at the man's face, leaving a gash below the right eye.

Payne hobbled to his feet, the pain in his back reducing his mobility. He grabbed the fallen bat and swung the hickory weapon across the man's left knee, shattering the patella.

The boulder erupted with splinters of rock shards as a cacophony of gunfire exploded through the forest. Payne darted behind the tree trunk to his left, his face stinging from the sweat trickling down onto the lacerations.

He glanced at the two groaning figures on the ground. The tattooed man was barely conscious, the back of his skull leaking blood where it had slammed into the boulder. The other brute was in a fetal position, clutching his shattered knee. Payne could see a Glock protruding from the man's waist.

So the spray-and-pray with automatic weapons must be plan B now that their amazing stealth attack has failed.

He leaned forward, smacking the nearest man on the neck with the bat, then retrieving the Glock. "Unless you want your brains scrambled, you're gonna tell me what I'm up against. How many more are out here?"

"Four, by the shitter."

Payne glanced around the side of the trunk, scanning the dense brush near the outhouse building, where he saw two men doing short bounds towards the campsite.

They must have been in hiding, waiting for Monroe to leave.

He partially pulled back the slide of the Glock 19, seeing the chamber was empty. Payne dropped out the mag, inspecting the fifteen full-metal-jacket rounds before reinserting it into the mag well. He vigorously pulled back the slide. "You know these things aren't worth shit without one in the pipe."

"Fuck you," said the henchman.

Payne drove the end of the bat like a pool stick into the man's face, knocking him out. He tossed the bat aside, then shimmied his way to a standing position, remaining behind the tree.

His options were to either trot down the slope and head into the woods or stay and fight. Four-on-one odds made him think the latter was out of the question.

Then he heard the sound of an approaching vehicle. The grumble of the engine was familiar. He glanced down the distant figure-eight loops in the road and saw Monroe's Bronco coming to a halt a hundred yards beyond the outhouse.

Damnit, she'll be cut to pieces.

Payne needed to draw the fire of his attackers now, before they could focus on the new threat. He zoomed in on the nearest figure, who had just sprung up behind a steel trash barrel and was moving towards the turnout for the campsite. Payne darted out, squeezing off three rounds before making it to the next tree. Two of the bullets hit their mark, striking the goon's right pec and sternum, dropping him on the road.

Payne glanced at the dead man, seeing it was the brawler in the vest from earlier.

The forest around Payne began splintering apart as another burst of gunfire strafed the trees. He grabbed the dead guy's AK-47 and dropped down the slope twenty feet, trotting along the base, then squat-walking back uphill to the campsite adjacent to his.

———

MERLE SCANNED the campground with his binoculars from a small berm a hundred yards outside the campground. He'd lost three of his six men in mere minutes, and now was worried that his remaining shooters would be stupid enough to open fire on the deputy.

Dumb bitch. She shoulda kept driving.

He pulled out his phone, firing off a frantic text to his guys to avoid engaging the deputy.

> Empty every round into Payne's location, then retreat to the van.

———

PAYNE HEARD another barrage of rounds slice through the air above his head, showering tree bark down on him. The remaining crew were shooting wildly now, and each wave of gunshots seemed a little farther off.

He crept out slightly from the fallen log near the road, seeing the last three shooters clumsily backpedaling through the shrubs only twenty yards from his location. He squeezed off two rounds from the AK, striking a portly thug in the belly. The man stumbled, then fell on his side.

Payne's hopes came through when the man's buddy returned to grab his friend by the collar and drag him out of the line of fire. Only he met the same fate, as Payne's rifle barked out two more rounds that struck the gangly figure in the collarbone and neck.

The bears are going to eat well out here tonight.

The last shooter sprayed his AK in a wild frenzy across three campsites.

Payne saw the back of the man's skull blow out before he dropped to the ground. He swept his gaze beyond the outhouse, seeing Monroe leaning out from the rear bumper of her Bronco with a scoped AR-15.

He heard the roar of a vehicle speeding away near the campground entrance and saw a white van spewing gravel as it raced east towards the highway.

Payne waited behind the log for a minute, scanning the campsite turned battlefield, until he was sure there were no more shooters. He stepped onto the road and quickly made his way to the nearest dead man, grabbing the AK.

"You good?" shouted Monroe from the protection afforded by her vehicle.

"Yeah. You?"

He made his way towards the other two shooters, picking up their rifles and removing the pistols from their beltlines. He backed up, setting the arsenal down on the cement pad around the outhouse as Monroe came up beside him. He noticed her shaking hands and wondered if this was the first time she'd discharged a service weapon.

"I called in to Hanson once I saw Merle's van parked nearby. There should be a bunch of county cops from the surrounding areas rolling in soon."

Payne patted the side of the AK. "All the same, I hope you don't mind if I hold on to this until they arrive."

She glanced at the dead men littering the campground. "I'd say you know a few things about military tactics, yet I didn't see anything in your records about past service."

"I spent a lot of time plinking squirrels when I was younger. Muscle memory always amazes me."

Monroe frowned. "Uh-huh, sure." The color faded from her face, and she braced a hand against a tree.

"You alright?" He glanced over her body for any signs of blood from being hit.

The deputy leaned over and began vomiting.

Payne moved closer, handing her a folded Kleenex from his back pocket.

"I'll be OK. I just need a minute." Monroe retched one more time, then stood and rested her shoulder against the oak.

Payne stepped back, scanning the campground and road again, then returning his gaze to the deputy, who was staring at the dead man with the blown-out skull.

Payne had no emotions, negative or positive, about killing these animals. They were targets that needed destroying, nothing more. But he knew Monroe had probably only slain cardboard targets at the range and that taking a life would leave an indelible mark on her soul. At least this time. The first time.

"Thanks," she said. Monroe balled and unballed her fists a few times, then shook her hands. "Goddamn shakes. You'd think I was on my fifth cup of coffee." She glanced at his steady hands, then up at his face.

He headed off her coming inquiry about his composure and pointed beyond his campsite. "There's two more guys near my hammock, whom you should probably cuff before they come around."

"You didn't plug them full of holes too?"

"I was unarmed at that point, in case you've forgotten." He nodded towards the entrance as they walked. "I'm assuming that Neanderthal from the jail was the shot-caller. That guy Merle."

"Probably. And knowing him, he'll be sticking to the back-roads, so we'll have to see if the county boys can get one of their fancy drones up in the air to spot him."

"Ah, shit."

She gave him a stern look, glancing over his torso. "What? You get hit?"

He shook his head in disgust, his eyes fixated on his Indian motorcycle and the black fluid leaking from a hole near the carburetor, along with the flattened rear tire. "Is there some mystical fucking force keeping me trapped in this region?"

Monroe gave a half-hearted chuckle. "I've asked myself that a few times over the years."

CHAPTER 13

WITHIN TWO HOURS, THE CAMPGROUND HAD TURNED INTO A full-blown crime scene with a SWAT team out of Redding and their forensics analysts, along with officers from ATF cordoning off the entire property.

After he and Monroe had given their statements to Hanson and the SWAT lieutenant, Payne took a seat at a vacant picnic table near the incident command post, which had hastily assembled around the patrol cars.

He sipped on a cup of coffee in a Styrofoam cup, watching the dozen or so officers and techs sweeping the ground for shell casings, photographing the bodies, and cataloguing the attackers' weapons.

The two injured men Payne had taken down by his hammock had been driven by ambulance to Redding. He was sure those brutes were going to be boosting the workload of the physical therapy department at whatever state penitentiary they eventually occupied.

Up until this morning, Payne's tour of the West Coast had been blissful and relaxing. Seeing the local attractions, camping under the stars, and meandering between coastal towns. It was a plan he continued to follow for the next few months or longer. As long as he lived frugally, he could subsist off his savings in this fashion for the next year if necessary, until the nomadic lifestyle no longer suited him.

Now, he had stacked up a few bodies, broken plenty of bones, and had ended up on a list of homicide suspects. Not to mention, a local meth kingpin was still on the loose, and Payne's motorcycle was out of commission for who knew how long.

And the day isn't even over yet.

Monroe finished talking with Hanson and walked over to the picnic table, resting one boot up on the bench across from Payne. "The sheriff said that he can comp you a room at the local motel across the street from our headquarters, so why don't I drive you back to town."

Payne gave her a puzzled look. "I thought Hanson hated me."

"He's a prick with everyone, especially new faces. That's just how he was baked in the oven."

"Huh?"

"Something my uncle used to say...about people being baked in God's oven and how everyone's got slightly different ingredients. It's goofy, I know."

"In the case of Merle, it'd be half-baked. Any word on that crack-pipe?"

Monroe shot a thumb over her shoulder towards the SWAT commander. "Drones found nothing, and the Forest Service guys haven't reported any sightings. Since Merle was a known weed and meth distributor around NorCal, he prob-ably linked up with one of the pot farms in the region and is hiding out at their place."

"And how is that a problem for a decked-out SWAT team? Those guys look like they could take down a city block in Fallujah."

"There are dozens of growers spread from here to the Oregon border, and they have multiple hideouts, some of which the DEA and state's drug task force don't even have mapped out because of the dense terrain and the numerous dirt roads crisscrossing the region. The nearest guy is McG, who has a cluster of weed plantations northwest of Absynth, but who knows if Merle is in league with him or working with one of the other growers south of here. It would take days for a tac team to comb through every ATV trail and dirt road in these parts, looking for that van."

It reminded him of the challenges he and his CIA team had encountered fighting insurgents in Pakistan, Afghanistan and Africa, where every valley was a maze of caves and booby-trapped trails, and the local fighters had all grown up knowing the escape routes, waterholes and best ambush sites.

He glanced at the crew out of Redding. "That would explain why the SWAT guys in such a sparsely populated region look as equipped as a SEAL team."

"And the pot industry is why so many people go missing in the Emerald Triangle in northern California."

"So it's not because of Sasquatch overlords enslaving people to work in their diamond mines?"

Monroe chuckled. "Jasper really got to you back in the holding cell. Talk about somebody who's smoked too much weed in his lifetime. He swears there's a UFO base hidden up in these hills."

"More like he was talking *at* me, trying to recruit a devotee into his fold."

She bent down, picking up a stick and coming around to his side. "The real culprits aren't extraterrestrials."

Monroe drew a crude map in the dirt, outlining the mountains and valleys around Absynth. She etched a sizable figure northwest of the town. "Every pot-growing area in the US has its own version of an emerald triangle. You stay out of this region and you'll be alright."

He traced his fingers along the five boundary lines she'd drawn. "This is more of a polygon, though, not a triangle."

She tossed the stick in his lap. "Shut up, smart-ass, or I'll reconsider the offer to drive you to the motel."

He stood, grabbing his cup and swigging down the remaining coffee. "So I get my own chauffeur again." He waved his hand towards the Bronco. "Just lead the way."

They walked past the bustle of officers around the command post. One of the men turned on a gas-powered generator, which activated the two dozen portable lights around the crime scene, giving the entire campground a stadium look. He paused by the Bronco, staring at his Indian motorcycle one last time, feeling like he was abandoning a faithful steed.

"There's a mechanic at the east end of Absynth who should be able to take care of your bike, assuming he can get out here tomorrow to pick it up in his trailer."

"Let's hope so." His shoulders slumped as he got inside the Bronco, sitting up front this time at Monroe's insistence. It didn't help knowing that his plans to race towards Oregon were thwarted and that the damage to his bike was not only going to be costly, but eat up the better part of a week, given the specialized parts that would have to be ordered.

As they drove through the campground towards the exit, Payne glanced over the splayed bodies. Some individuals in the spec-ops community kept a tally of how many people they'd killed over the course of their career. Payne was never one of those guys, but he was sure it went far beyond double digits, and this evening's body count blurred into the shrouded figures he kept tamped down in the jagged land-scape of his memory.

CHAPTER 14

AFTER EVA LEFT HER FRIEND BETHANY'S APARTMENT AT MIDDAY, she drove to Jitters Coffee Shop, eager to speak with Gabe about her brother's findings. Two cups of coffee and an hour later, she was still waiting. Gabe hadn't responded to her texts or calls, and she wasn't sure if he'd overslept or had forgotten.

Except he said whatever Aaron had discovered was "big, really big."

She tried his office number, but it went straight to voice-mail. Eva glanced at the sidewalks, hoping to see him strolling in, apologetic, because he'd rushed out his apartment door after realizing he was late. But Gabe Joyce was nowhere to be seen amongst the blur of pedestrians.

She tapped her fingers on the side of the table, the namesake of the café exacting its toll on her nervous system.

Eva grabbed her shoulder bag and headed for the door. Though it was on the other side of the city, she still had a narrow window to make it to Gabe's office. Maybe she would find him there, or at least be able to inquire with his colleagues regarding his whereabouts. After that, she'd grab a hotel room nearby and plot out her next move. Without Gabe to fill her in on what Aaron was involved with, she was running blind.

Where the hell are you, Gabe?

She repeated the same cursed question again, but with her brother's name inserted at the end, feeling like the sidewalk was crumbling beneath her feet with each step.

———

WAGNER WALKED through the alley with his ball cap pulled down and his head low. Crossing the street, he got into the passenger's front seat of the black Suburban.

"She give up anything?" asked Schulz, who was sitting behind the wheel.

"Nothing we didn't already know," replied Wagner, who had removed his boot knife and was flicking off the water droplets after he'd rinsed it free of arterial blood in Bethany Harkins' kitchen. He leaned back, staring at the skyscrapers in the distance. "Although, she did mention something that might be of help."

"About Eva or Aaron?" inquired Simon Regal, the man in the back seat, who had a neatly groomed black beard.

"It appears Aaron had a small lab somewhere in Absynth where he did his research."

"The security guys at the Wayland site said Daly only had a small home in town," said Schulz.

Wagner shook his head. "This is something different. The woman made it sound like it was a cabin or shack outside of town."

"Makes sense given the guy was into bugs," said Elke, a slender female operative in the back seat behind the driver. She slid forward, handing him a tablet, which showed a red dot slowly moving along Interstate 5. "The tracker I placed on

Eva's vehicle is showing she just got on the southbound. The only thing of interest in that direction is that guy Gabe's workplace, so she might be heading there."

Wagner motioned for Schulz to drive. "Bethany said that, unless Eva heard something from Gabriel Joyce to change her mind, she was going to Absynth to find out what's going on with her brother."

"That's going to be a long eight-hour drive," said the bearded man. "Probably not something she's going to pull off tonight."

Elke fastened her seatbelt. "If we were back in Europe, we'd cross through four other countries in that time. I can't believe how big this fucking state is."

"Let's keep our tail on her. If it comes to it, we'll follow her north to Absynth, but that's going to eat up a lot of time," said Wagner, gazing at the skyline. "I was hoping we could wrap this up here, but my gut is beginning to tell me otherwise."

CHAPTER 15

PAYNE HAD SLEPT FITFULLY IN THE DINGY MOTEL ROOM. THE sagging bed had left spring marks on his ribs, making him appreciate his hammock even more. He was pretty sure the Caboose Motel had been built when the railway was first put in over a century ago.

After showering and getting dressed, Payne called the mechanic's shop on the edge of town and checked on the status of his motorcycle. The owner was heading out to the campground in the afternoon to load the Indian onto his trailer and then would get back with Payne once he'd been able to work out an estimate for repairs.

Payne tried to shrug off his irritation by going for a short walk. Eventually, his appetite for breakfast steered him down the street to the café Monroe had mentioned as being the crown jewel of Absynth.

He glanced at the lopsided sign hanging over the faded wood façade. *More like cheap zirconium.*

The place was hopping, and he waited in line while glancing over at the other patrons, who were a mix of locals in jeans and Carhartt jackets or hikers with pricey boots and the garb to match.

When his turn at the counter arrived, he ordered a straight black coffee and an egg and ham burrito.

"You sure you don't want a cappuccino or latte?" said the older man behind the counter, whose accent differed from the other locals he'd met.

"I'll stick with the basics, thanks. That gonna be a problem?"

The man pursed his lips, grabbing a beige mug off the rack and sliding it towards Payne. "Nah, just seems like everybody wants one of the fancy drinks."

Payne noticed a fraternal order of police ring on the left hand. He gazed up at the wall, seeing a host of framed photos, one of which showed the guy in a police uniform beside a fifty-something woman. "Were you an LEO in these parts?"

The man gave him a pleased look as he reached under the counter and pulled out a plate and utensils. "Retired after twenty-two years as a cop down in LA. Moved up here with the wife a few years back." He waved his hand at the dining area. "She always wanted to have her own café."

"Well, she chose wisely. This seems like a goldmine."

The man lowered his eyes as a deflated look came over him. He turned, handing the written order to the line cook to his rear, then rang up the order on the cash register.

Before Payne could pull out the cash from his pocket, a twenty-dollar bill slid along the counter towards the owner. "This one's on me," said Deputy Kessel, who moved up alongside Payne. "Consider it an apology for the way I conducted myself yesterday."

Payne shuffled to the left, glancing at the man's face, which seemed to hold a genuine expression. "Well, I appreciate that, thanks."

"Least I could do." Kessel leaned in, placing an order for a caramel macchiato and a blueberry Danish.

After paying, the deputy pivoted around. "There's someone I'd like you to meet. He said you two already spoke on the phone a few weeks ago."

Kessel led Payne to a corner table where an older man with a thick gray beard was sitting. With his faded cowboy boots and leathery skin, he looked like he belonged in an Old West museum. He was framed by shelves of local jewelry and ceramics for sale behind him.

"Mr. Payne, this is Tommy Larkin."

The older man stood, extending a hand as the two exchanged courtesies.

"This is a pleasant surprise."

"Likewise, young fella." Larkin sat and used his boot to push out a chair near Payne.

"I'll leave you guys to it. I gotta get my order and run," said Kessel as he departed.

Larkin shoved a forkful of eggs into his mouth. "I was looking forward to meeting you after everything you told me about growing up with a dad who was a game warden and all the wildlife in northern Michigan."

"You have a good memory. You must talk to a lot of people, given your reputation."

"Oh, what reputation is that?"

"Not many people can claim they've been face-to-face with hundreds of cougars in their lifetime."

"Ah, yeah, those were some amazing times. But it was probably only about eighty or so cats."

"Oh, is that all?" said Payne with a chuckle.

"Back when there was an increase in human fatalities around places like LA and San Fran, I was called in to track the maneaters and put 'em down. After that, I worked with cougar biologists out of the universities who needed someone to help in the field with tranquilizing cats so they could radio collar 'em."

"Hell, I was always thrilled to find black bear or the occasional wolf track. Only a few documented cougar sightings in the Upper Peninsula, but I never saw one. I'm sure looking forward to learning more from you."

"Well, I hate to break this to ya, but I was just making calls to the other participants in our tracking class when Deputy Kessel told me you were here. Unfortunately, I had to cancel this weekend's event on account of the storm rolling in. Not much tracking that can be done in the kinda rain and goopy mud we're in store for."

This just keeps getting better. Why do I feel like this town has its own plans for me?

"Becky, I mean Deputy Monroe, told me about what happened at the campground and all the troubles you've had since arriving. I want to extend an offer to stay in one of the cabins at the field station north of town until next weekend. You can have access to my tracking library and plaster casts, as well as the camp kitchen and shower house. Other than the caretaker, who won't be back for a few days, you'll have the place to yourself. Beats stayin' in one of the fleabag motels in town."

Payne sighed. He'd seen photos online of the field station and the lush valley surrounding it. Plus, being able to sift through Larkin's collection of books and research would be priceless. "That's very hospitable. I don't mind paying, or if you want to put me to work on the property, I can do that too."

He waved his shovel-like hand in the air. "No need, son. Although, if this storm is the doozy they're saying it is, I might need help clearing some trees off the road after it's all over."

"Deal."

Larkin gulped down the last of his coffee and dragged a napkin across his beard. "I gotta run home and tend to my horses, but I still got your number and will text you directions and the codes for the lockbox on the main gate and the other buildings."

The two men stood, exchanging handshakes again before Larkin donned his black cowboy hat off a peg on the wall. He thrust his chin at the front entrance. "Seems like someone else is looking for you."

Payne turned and saw Monroe walking towards him. She paused briefly to speak with the owner and grab an order off the counter, then headed to the back table.

Larkin tipped his hat at her as he walked past while she responded with a smile. Payne wasn't sure if he was imagining it, but it seemed like her smile continued to grow as she moved closer.

"From the looks of it, this place is the main office for the sheriff's department, not the building across the street."

"Haha. I see you've progressed from just being a smart-ass to a court jester."

"It's a significant step up in social standing, and with better hours." Payne glanced at the kitchen, eager for breakfast. "That guy behind the counter was a cop, eh? Is that why you and Kessel come here…for the generous LEO discount?"

Monroe pulled out a chair and sat. "Yeah, Earl's a good guy. His wife died last year, leaving him tied to this place. He keeps talking about selling, but I don't think he has the heart for it. Too much of her in these walls. Besides, he's told me more than a few times that he's stuck for the next year with the lease on this place."

He gazed at her tiny coffee cup. "And what are you drinking?"

"Cortado."

"What the hell is that?"

"One shot of espresso with one part steamed milk and a dash of foam on top."

"You know, a cup of coffee probably has more kick and costs far less than what you paid for that designer foo-foo."

"Straight black coffee is for people lacking sophistication. Plus, it tastes like motor oil." She slid the half-empty cup towards him. "Try some."

He pushed it back, using a fork. "No, thank you."

Monroe cradled the diminutive cup, glancing over her shoulder at the employees behind the counter. "I used to work as a barista down in Redding when I was going to college."

She pointed to the three stainless-steel apparatuses behind the counter. "Those espresso machines each cost twenty thousand apiece. They are finely engineered devices that force hot, pressurized water through the espresso grounds to give it a flavor and texture unlike anything you can get from regular coffee." She emitted a girlish smile. "I'm kind of an espresso snob."

"And I pegged you for just a regular snob."

She frowned. "You're quite the comedian."

"So you weren't always a country bumpkin."

She sipped her diminutive drink. "Even though it's only around ninety thousand people, Redding is the big city for everyone in NorCal. The next largest is Sacramento, but that's almost a three-hour drive. And everyone growing up in Absynth wants to escape to a city…any city."

"Was it the small-town atmosphere and locals that drew you back here?"

Monroe shrugged her shoulders. "A little of both, maybe. I also have aunts and uncles and cousins, and, of course, my nephews are here." She glanced around the café, then out the front windows. "Used to be, until this year at least, that the main concern was rowdy tourists at the campgrounds during the summer or drunks during the weekend festivals down-town. Now, not so much."

"What changed?"

She swiveled in her chair, glancing over the other patrons before speaking, lowering her voice. "There've been half a dozen missing people, mostly in the backcountry. We usually get a call a week or two after they've been through here from their families, saying that this was the last place they were at."

"Hikers?"

"A few, but mainly just people like you, passing through or camping outside of town."

"And their bodies never turn up?"

She shook her head.

"When I was reading up on the wildlife in this area, I saw that there had been a lot of cougar telemetry studies done here because of the cat population. But I reckon a guy like Larkin would know all about that."

She shook her head more fervently this time. "Nah, I've been over that with Tommy. We discussed the bear and cougar predation angle, but he ruled that out, saying there would be some obvious physical signs along the trails where these folks were last known to have been. Plus, those critters normally don't lose their taste for people once they become maneaters, so there would be an increase in attacks."

"Sounds about right. What, then?" He stroked the side of his cup. "That strange dude with the Sasquatch stories said something about a ghost in the woods. Said it was a vengeful spirit that came after the wicked, or some bullshit like that."

She flared an eyebrow. "And you believed him? Maybe you're not as sharp as I thought."

"Folktales and superstitions always have their origins in something practical. For example, the Inuit in the Arctic have stories about a supernatural creature that wanders the land at night, looking for children to eat. It might seem like just a campfire story, by our standards, but that tale used to prevent small kids from stepping outside the igloo at night where it's fifty below zero and death from hypothermia could happen in minutes."

Payne glanced up into her eyes. "This guy in the holding cell with me also said the ghost was new in these parts. Considering you just had a bullet-riddled body show up on your turf and an increase in missing people, maybe you've got a vigilante on your hands."

She looked at the time on her iPhone. "Interesting theory, but please keep it to yourself. I don't need the rest of Absynth getting any more spooked than they already are."

Monroe finished her cortado and stood. "I've gotta run. I need to finish closing a few backcountry roads before this storm rolls in this weekend." She gave him a scrutinizing glare. "What trouble are you going to get into today?"

He leaned back, folding his arms. "I envision more coffee and some reading in my day."

"Uh-huh, sure. Just be good, Payne."

"I'll take your advice to heart, Deputy."

He watched her leave, her confident stride causing his eyes to linger on her through the windows as she walked across the street.

A few seconds later, the owner came over, setting down a coffee pitcher on the table along with a breakfast burrito. "Apologies for the delay on your meal. Got a new kid on the grill who thinks being slow is a lifestyle." Earl patted the coffee pitcher. "Bottomless cups are on me, so finish this off."

The owner glanced at Monroe in the distance, then turned towards Payne. "She's a pit bull, but with heart. I've seen a lot of women cops in my day, and she's one of the good ones."

"Seems like it." He decided to probe the man for his take

on things. "Seems like the entire sheriff's department has some dedicated folks."

Earl withdrew the dishrag off his shoulder and wiped up the crumbs on the table. "Every orchard has at least one sour apple."

Payne gave him a puzzled look. "Meaning?"

"Meaning just that. Even in a one-pony town like Absynth, there's always somebody who puts his own agenda over what he was elected to do."

"You talking about Hanson?"

Earl nodded, flinging the towel back on his shoulder. "I'm just glad that rickety old dog is retiring soon. Make room for a new generation." He glanced out at Monroe again. "Some younger blood on the police force is what this place needs."

Payne glanced beyond the man at the shelf full of local artwork containing handmade red ceramics. "By chance, do you know the individual who made that pottery?"

Earl glanced at the row of items, then out towards the front window. "Paige did. Her gallery's two blocks east of here. Quirky gal, but she's an artist, after all."

"You don't pull any punches, do you?"

"Why would I? If a person's got something on their mind, they should just spit it out instead of dancing around how they really feel about something."

"Can't argue with that."

Earl moved to the empty table to the right, collecting the empty breakfast plates and bantering with the other customers.

After he left, Payne stood and examined the pottery. It was made from the same red clay he'd seen on the dead man's boots.

He returned to his seat, quickly devouring his burrito and swigging down another cup of black coffee.

When he finished, Payne exited the establishment,

peering down Main Street at the row of shops. He spotted the sign for Paige's Red Valley Pottery right where Earl said it would be.

With his motorcycle awaiting lengthy repairs and with nothing much to do in Absynth, he thought he would do some investigating of his own.

He wanted to clear himself of being a suspect and also wondered why Monroe was giving him such a long leash, acting like his pal, as was Kessel, who had seemingly flipped off his asshat switch for the morning.

Payne saw his reflection in the windshield of a Chevy truck parked at the curb. His beard and shaggy hair could use a trim. He figured it might mean getting hassled less in small towns with idle cops.

He glanced at his scruffy image again and dismissed the idea of cleaning up his image.

I'm living by my own rules. Otherwise, what's the point of being a freewheeling nomad?

He glanced at the sheriff's department again, recalling the photo of Monroe's brother in her office. He pulled out his iPhone and called one of the three numbers in his address book.

A woman answered. "Kyle, are you actually calling me again? This is the fourth time in twelve months. We must really be friends."

"Funny, Alisa. I miss you too."

"You already getting bored with sleeping on the beach and watching solar eclipses from a mountain bungalow?"

"I think we have very different images of what the care-free life looks like."

Alisa Fairbanks had served as the intelligence analyst and targeter for the CIA and had been Payne's eyes and ears during missions abroad for nearly a decade. She seemed much happier since being in the private sector, where her cyber-skills were used for managing the computer defenses of several Fortune 500 companies.

"So where you at these days?" she asked.

"Absynth, California, though I could just as easily say a dark crater on the moon."

"That much fun, eh?"

"You don't know the half of it. It's an epic story for another time, but right now I was wondering if you might be able to look into something for me."

"As in a major project or just someone's unlisted address?"

"Neither, but it's not major, I don't think, anyway."

"Shoot."

"There's an army soldier named Derek Monroe from Absynth. He was an Army Ranger who died in the line of duty, but his family, a lady I know, who is his sister, hasn't been able to get any answers on the where and how part. I realize you may not be able to unearth the latter, but just knowing where he died would be a big help for her and his wife."

"Is that last name with a *U* or an *O*?"

"Two *O*'s, and he apparently died last year at this time."

"I'll see what I can do. Shouldn't take too long. I have a friend who's married to an Army Ranger, but I'll also do some digging of my own."

"Thanks."

"Enjoy your weekend, Kyle and I want to hear the juicy details on your trip sometime soon, including this new woman you're doing favors for."

"It's not like that."

"Sure. Like I said, can't wait for the details."

After she hung up, he slid the phone back in his pocket and made his way to the pottery shop, hoping his curiosity would pay off so he didn't have to languish in the café the entire weekend.

CHAPTER 16

MATT GRAVES GRABBED HIS COFFEE THERMOS AS HE DEPARTED HIS house, hopping on his ATV and driving across the twenty-acre property to a faded red barn in the southwest corner.

He noted the familiar sight of three pickup trucks where he'd seen them last night, but noting the white Chevy van caused his blood pressure to spike.

McG pushed open the double doors on the side of the immense barn and stepped in; the odor of dried cannabis and burnt steel pierced his nostrils. While the majority of his cannabis crop would be harvested in a few weeks, there were several sun-dominant valleys at lower elevations that had already been cut and were hanging in bundles from the rafters.

In the far left corner was his second-in-command, Toko, who was welding a new hitch on a recently built trailer while three other men were unboxing bundles of bailing twine and spools of cellophane.

This structure was the epicenter of his operations, and since partnering with Wayland, whose soil scientists had helped further his crop yield, his barn was about to be brimming with floor-to-rafter bundles of pot. Half of the crop would spend three weeks drying here while the remainder would be spread around the numerous outbuildings dotting the property.

Toko turned off the spot welder and removed his visor. Though the five-foot-two Filipino weighed three times less than McG, he was a formidable fighter, having worked for years as an enforcer for a dope operation out of McG's old hometown in LA.

His physical stature and unassuming expression made people underestimate him, which worked to his advantage. Given the man's propensity for using blades to solve his problems, Graves was sure Toko always had half a dozen knives hidden on his body.

McG glanced at the disheveled figure of Merle passed out on a bale of straw to the right.

"He hasn't moved an inch since he collapsed there around midnight," said Toko, who removed his welder's apron and leather gloves. "He looked pretty hopped up on something when he rolled in. And it was just him. When I asked about the rest of his guys, he said they were all dead, killed in some turf battle or some shit."

Graves sighed, kicking Merle's dirty sneakers. When the man didn't budge, Graves placed his boot on Merle's chest and shoved him back, causing him to topple off the bale.

"What the fuck?" snapped Merle, hopping up and reaching for the lock blade in his pocket. He paused when he saw who was standing before him.

"Where's the rest of your crew?" said Graves.

Merle scratched his bristly chin. "Picked apart, man. They got wasted by this dude who rolled into town the other day."

Graves shot a glance at Toko, both of them possessing puzzled expressions. "The hell you mean? Who?" said Graves.

"Some guy named Payne. He crossed one of my crew outside of town, talking shit and throwing his weight around. When we went over to simmer things down, Payne goes ape-shit and starts shootin'. Dropped some of my guys, then another and another, just like that." He snapped his wispy fingers.

McG glanced over the man's face and clothing. "But you got away without a scratch."

"I was takin' a leak when it all went down, man. Before I know it, I see this lady cop roll up. That's when I bugged out." He pulled up his sagging jeans. "But don't worry, man, I took a crazy-ass, winding route to get here. No way anyone could've followed me."

Toko folded his arms, gazing at his boss. "That probably explains why our scouts to the south reported drones in the sky yesterday evening."

"My contact mentioned a shitload of police units out of Redding blazing through town yesterday evening," said Graves.

Toko glared at Merle. "What'd this guy, Payne, look like?"

Merle's eyes darted along the ground. "Black beard, tall like McG, and kinda shaggy hair. Drove a motorcycle. An old one by the looks of it."

Toko gave McG an uneasy glance. "Sounds like the same guy at the campground that we set up for Daly's murder. Dude looked like a drifter."

"Yeah, that bastard was at the campground west of town," Merle said sheepishly.

The Filipino stepped closer, resting his hand on a fixed blade on his hip. "Your showdown with Payne happened at the campground? That's a helluva long way from town. And it's down a dead-end road, which means you must have followed him there."

"Was that before or after you were arrested for harassing women in Absynth, you asshole?" asked McG.

Merle bit his cracked lips. "Payne crossed the line with me and my guys. He had it coming."

McG shook his head. He leaned forward, setting his thermos down, then swiftly grabbing Merle's greasy black hair and yanking his head back. "Do you know how long my family operation has been in this valley? How long it's managed to stay below the fucking radar all these years?"

"No, man. But it's cool. Everything's cool. I wasn't followed here."

"Shut up." McG twisted the man's skull, staring into the gaunt, bloodshot eyes. "I'm allowing you to live for now because I still need your connections down in SoCal, but I'm beginning to rethink our arrangement."

Merle waved his hands frantically. "I'll do my next three runs at my expense. You won't have to pay me at all, man."

"With what crew?" McG shoved the man back into some fuel drums.

Merle stumbled to the ground, emitting a whimper.

McG stepped back, wiping his hand on his jeans, then grabbing his thermos and glancing at Toko. "Have one of the guys get him cleaned up. He smells like horse piss. And stow his van in the barn in case any drones are still operating around the mountain."

"You want me to look further into this guy Payne?" asked Toko.

"No, I'll take care of it. If this guy's hanging around Absynth, my informant will know all about him."

CHAPTER 17

PAYNE STEPPED INTO THE POTTERY STORE, HIS EYES IMMEDIATELY watering from the incense burning in a conch shell resting on a nearby windowsill.

The place reminded him of the interior of an old saloon in a Western movie. The paneling looked like it was milled from local timber, and the weathered floorboards creaked with each step. Even the windows looked like they were made of antique glass, and a pot-bellied woodstove was sitting in the corner on a sandstone slab.

A chunky yellow Labrador retriever resting beside the back counter lifted its head and peered at Payne, then lay down again, having assessed the new arrival.

"Bosco only comes bounding over if you have a treat, so don't take it personally," said a woman's voice from behind a beaded curtain to the rear of the counter. She finished stuffing the remnants of a donut into her mouth, then dragged a sleeve across her lips.

"You Paige?"

She poked her head out, glancing at him. "That's me. What can I do ya for?"

He scanned the floor-to-ceiling shelves lining three walls, marveling at the sheer amount of handmade clay mugs, bowls, vases, serving dishes and animal figurines. And all of it with the same red hue that he'd seen on the dead man's boots.

"Earl from the café said you had fashioned the pottery that was for sale in his place."

She smiled, aiming a thumb back at herself as she walked out from behind the curtains. "That's me. Everything from scratch. And I do it in the old way, well, mostly the old-fashioned way, by collecting the raw materials and adding the temper, to shaping everything by hand. No pottery wheels in my place." Her shoulders slumped slightly. "But I do use a kiln for the firing process."

"You say that like it's a bad thing."

Paige glanced over his face for a moment. "Only if you're a purist. Some folks think that because I gather my own clay and do everything by hand, I should put all the completed pieces in a firepit out back and finish the process like the natives did." She leaned both of her forearms on the counter. "I used to do it that way, but, my God, that eats up so much time, and I got other things to do if I'm gonna keep this place afloat."

Payne was surprised by her openness and wondered if she was going to reveal her astrology sign and favorite ice cream next. Not that he minded. He found it refreshing, but he had spent so many years in an occupation that fostered deception and hidden agendas that he still found it odd to converse openly with a complete stranger.

"Well, my hat goes off to you for being so immersed in your craft that you even collect your own clay. I imagine that has to be a unique selling point."

She flared her eyebrows. "Yes and no. Every artist has to have an angle. I guess that's mine. Always has been. I never liked that shiny, glazed pottery that looks like it was made in a factory."

She glanced at his footwear, then up at his face again before stepping out from behind the counter. Paige walked to the shelf on the right and pulled down a ceramic canteen. It was disk-shaped with carry loops on the side as if they had emerged that way. "This one might suit you, being you seem like an outdoor kinda guy."

"Do I?"

She smiled again, but it exuded warmth, not the plastic charm of a salesperson.

He palmed the container, examining the elegant contours and pleasing design. "This reminds me of the old metal canteens used by the US cavalry during the Geronimo Campaign in Arizona."

"Wow, interesting. I got the idea after seeing some ceramic vessels in an Indian museum down near Palm Springs years ago." She leaned against an upright wooden beam. "That where you're from…Arizona?"

"No, far from it, but I sure like the Southwest." He glanced at the price tag as she looked at her dog, assuring himself it was within his budget and reminding himself the purchase was a form of payoff for local information, which he needed to further his personal inquiries.

He moved to the counter, placing the canteen on it, then kneeled to pet Bosco on his back leg, noticing the familiar red residue on the dog's nails and paws.

"And this fella here looks like he goes on collecting trips with you."

She knelt by the Lab's head, stroking his face. "The yard out back is full of clay, and he's always digging in it, trying to catch mice or pocket gophers."

"Why's it so red? I've only seen that kind of color in rocks around Sedona or Monument Valley."

"Two percent iron oxide. It's basically rusted rock. The natural color is actually kind of sandy-brown, but the iron oxide has leached out onto the substrate over millions of years and given it that beautiful red appearance." Paige waved her hands through the air as she spoke, like she was in front of a classroom of apt geology students.

He was taken with her passion for her art as much as he was with her unique blend of Western and Bohemian fashion.

Payne stood, resting his hand on the canteen. "So I'll take this but wondered if I could pay for it now and come back for it when I'm ready to leave town in a few days."

She rested an elbow on the counter, twirling a strand of honey-blonde hair. "You got it."

Payne removed his wallet, pulling out a fifty and a twenty. "Just out of curiosity, where did you find red clay like this? I've been traveling and camping around these parts, and all I've seen is black dirt."

"Only two places around Absynth…down Highway 3 there's an old bridge over McMurty Creek. About a half mile south of there is a good deposit; and there's also a cutout along the banks of Templeton River a hundred yards or so from the Beachum Gulch Trailhead."

She leaned in closer. "However, the purest clay that I use comes from a place many miles from here, but only Bosco and I know where, and neither of us are gonna give up that spot."

He glanced down at the dog, who lifted his head at the sound of his name. "Yeah, you look like you have unquestioning loyalty, old boy."

Payne glanced at Paige, feeling like he needed one other critical asset. "Last question: where's the nearest rental car place?"

CHAPTER 18

AFTER RENTING A SUBARU FORESTER FROM HERTZ, PAYNE stopped by the grocery store and loaded up on some water bottles, jerky and a few apples before heading out of town.

The drive south on Highway 3 was like something out of a postcard. The snowcapped peaks of the Trinity Alps framed the western horizon on Payne's right while occasional breaks in the forest on the left provided a glimpse of endless mountain ranges extending to the horizon. In between both ranges was an undulating ocean of pine and spruce forests intersected by McMurty Creek, which wove itself alongside the road.

With no other vehicles in his rearview mirror for the past ten minutes, Payne felt like he was the last man on Earth and relished the solitude.

Eight miles later, he arrived at a turnoff south of the bridge that Paige had indicated. Payne slowed the Subaru and made a left turn onto a Forest Service road whose faded signage was barely visible.

He'd told himself earlier that this was just an exploratory

trip to satisfy his curiosity about the clay found on the dead man's boots, and with the coming storm, any tracks would be swept away, so this was his only chance to search the area. Since he was unarmed and in unfamiliar territory, he would turn around if anything raised his hackles.

The hard-packed road was barely wide enough for one vehicle, and he hoped he wouldn't encounter anyone coming from the other direction, though the lack of tire marks made him think few people ventured down this route. The online information he'd read about the region indicated this was a seasonal road kept open for hikers and hunters heading to Scott Mountain.

After only a half mile, the road became rutted and required maneuvering to avoid grounding out the Forester. Five minutes later, he pulled off on a dirt shoulder on the right that overlooked the meandering river below. To the left was a meadow carpeted with blue lupine that extended a quarter mile to the base of a large hill, which stood like a sentinel over the region.

Payne exited the vehicle, grabbing his daypack and donning a ball cap. The only sounds were the wind through the pines and the babble of the river below. Upon further inspection, it appeared to be more of a creek with ankle-deep water the color of tea.

A small trail descended thirty feet below, where there was an old campfire ring of soot-blackened rocks littered with crushed beer cans.

So much for Leave No Trace.

He made his way down the slope, recalling the vague directions he'd received from the potter. Payne figured even if he didn't locate the clay source, any time spent under open skies made for a good day. Given how much there was to learn about the natural world, there was no such thing as a wasted day on the trail. At least, that was what his father always said, and he was seldom wrong about things pertaining to the wilds.

Payne lingered a moment around the derelict campfire ring, noticing an absence of tracks and the pockmarked dirt from the last time it rained. He continued past the former party scene and made his way along the narrow trail that skirted the left side of the creek, eventually hopping across some flat rocks towards the other embankment.

The creek looked like it followed the contours of the road heading south. Or more likely that the original builders had followed the creek contours. To the right, the forest sloped gently up towards a rocky escarpment of dark gray basalt that muscled its way up from the ground. At the base of the rock formation were numerous overhangs, which looked like they could provide an expedient shelter.

The next mile of hiking was through knee-high ferns that choked the trail, and there was little evidence of any creatures other than deer traveling this pathway. Nor did the riparian area reveal any clay outcroppings along the creek bed, and Payne wondered if Paige had intentionally misled him.

He pictured the free-spirited woman sipping coffee beside her window and watching the other tourists mill around town, while grinning about the one she'd sent on a wild-goose chase.

It was just then that he rounded the bend in the trail and saw a slick outcropping of red clay on the opposite side of the creek. The substrate had a greasy sheen and seemed to bleed out from the embankment. Payne made his way down to the creek bed, studying the ground, but the surface only revealed a plethora of deer and raccoon tracks.

He gazed at the forest on the other side, not seeing any obvious route in from that direction. Payne retraced his steps back up to the trail, then glanced in the opposite direction from his rental vehicle but didn't see indications that anyone had ventured this way.

With hunger gnawing at him, he removed his pack and pulled out a Clif Bar and a bottled water. While snacking, he took in the tranquil setting, imagining a distant time a few centuries earlier when the Wintu, Shasta and Kurok tribes lived here, fishing in this creek, foraging for wild plants, and hunting throughout the countryside.

Suddenly his prepackaged food seemed less appealing. While scanning the basalt formation on a ridgeline to his right, he noticed a small cave.

Exactly the kind of place to look for prehistoric rock art.

He finished his last bite and washed it down with the remaining water, then put the empty bottle back in his pack and trudged up the slope towards the fish-mouth opening of the rock shelter.

For the first time in years, he felt a sense of excitement at exploring a cave for its intrinsic value rather than seeing it as a potential threat for harboring insurgents like he and his team had done countless times in Afghanistan and Africa.

Payne reached the lip and paused to let his eyes adjust to the darkness. The cave was just over two feet taller than his six-foot stature and extended back ten feet. The jagged ceiling was sooty from years of campfires, and the remnants of charred logs covered in cobwebs sat dormant in a small depression in the center. The damp air smelled like a barn as the stench of rodent and bat droppings wafted out from the cave whenever the wind stirred.

He removed his flashlight and scanned the walls on either side but, to his disappointment, didn't see any petroglyphs.

The wind outside had increased, creating a small vortex of dead leaves along the cave walls. But just beyond the periphery of his hearing, there was no mistaking the sickeningly familiar sound of metal on metal behind him, and he knew someone had just racked a rifle.

Payne pivoted slowly away from the entrance, staring at two barefoot men pointing AK-47s at his chest.

CHAPTER 19

FOR A SECOND, PAYNE WONDERED IF HE HAD STEPPED BACK A century in time given the appearance of the two forest-dwellers. Their shaggy hair and unkempt beards were accentuated by their deeply tanned skin. Tattered shirts accompanied their cut-off jeans, and their legs were peppered with old lacerations. Both of them appeared to be in their mid-twenties, and it was clear they had an aversion to bathing in creek water.

Payne raised both hands. "Easy, fellas." It was then that he noticed the lush flora growing alongside the man on the right. He had been so focused on the cave during his ascent that he'd missed the clusters of marijuana plants dotting the hillside at this elevation.

"Hand over your ID," barked the skinny figure on the left, his yellow teeth glaring out beyond his cracked lips.

"Look, I'm just exploring the area for rock-art sites."

The thin man stepped forward, thrusting his AK out and glancing down at Payne's pockets. "Don't make me ask again, old man."

The foul-smelling brute was standing close enough so the barrel was only a few inches from Payne's sternum.

They must want to know if I'm local or not.

Payne figured that if it was the former, then these guys wouldn't want to draw attention from the sheriff's department when a missing person report was filed compared with that of an outsider who could be buried in the boonies without much concern.

The man shook his head. "With all the places in this region, you thought a little day hike up this no-name creek would be a good place to snap off a few pictures for your Instagram account, eh?"

"It's actually listed as McMurty Creek on the map and the signs." Payne slowly slid his hand down to his BDU pocket on the right and undid the Velcro before removing his wallet. He pulled out Monroe's business card and gave it to the steely-eyed man.

He glanced at the wording. "What the fuck is this?" The man handed it back to his friend while keeping the AK steady.

"Thought you should get acquainted with the deputy since you'll both be meeting her soon," said Payne.

"Fuck this guy; he's gotta be a fed working with the county cops," said the burly man to the rear while he scanned the creek bed below.

"Hand over the wallet, old-timer," said the skinny guy, who shoved the barrel into Payne's chest.

He did a hasty inspection of the AK, seeing the safety was on. "You two may be younger than me, but I have twice your fighting experience."

Payne flung the wallet at the man's face, then pivoted sideways and yanked the rifle barrel down with his right hand while sending a vicious back fist into the man's nose. Cartilage and bone snapped, sending a rivulet of blood along the thug's chin. Payne twisted the rifle, then sent the barrel straight back into the guy's face, causing him to lose his footing and stumble back into his accomplice.

Both goons tumbled down the slope, crashing through the cannabis.

Payne retrieved his wallet from the ground and grabbed his driver's license from where it had fallen, then trotted down the hill, pausing to pick up the other AK. He did a quick chamber check on both weapons as he approached the two groaning figures.

"You broke my fucking arm, asshole," shouted the big man, who was clutching his left forearm, which had a swollen lump below the elbow.

"Better than a broken leg, which would make walking out of here a helluva lot more challenging."

The thin man rolled on his side, reaching for a fixed blade on his belt.

Payne closed the gap, slamming his boot down on the wrist, which made the sound of snapping twigs.

The man recoiled against a tree, screaming in pain.

"Now, you and your buddy can sign each other's casts," said Payne as he bent over and removed the blade, sticking it into a tree behind him.

"McG is gonna crucify you, motherfucker," said the burly man as he sat up and leaned back against a mossy stump.

"With such a fear-inducing name like that, I'm assuming that's your boss?"

The man with the bad teeth bleated back, "You on McG's turf out here, man, and he don't take lightly to trespassers."

Payne kicked some dirt in the guy's face. "Pretty sure this is my land since it's Forest Service, which means it's federal, which means it's supported by my tax dollars, genius." He waved the barrel at the man's face. "Either of you guys twitch, and I'll dump a few rounds into your kneecaps. Got it?"

The big man gave a faint nod while the other one shot out the middle finger from his good hand. He started to stand, but Payne squeezed off two rounds into the tree trunk above his head, splintering bark down on the man's face. "Got it?"

The goon ducked down, coiling into a fetal position. "Alright, goddammit."

Payne removed his iPhone and called 911. He had to retreat a few feet back up the hill to get a clear signal, but once he started explaining the situation to an exasperated Monroe, he was pretty sure he'd be facing another round of questioning back in her office.

———

An hour later, McG watched through binoculars from the distant hillside across the meadow as the female deputy handcuffed his two men and placed them in the back of her vehicle.

Monroe; not like her to venture off the pavement.

With his refrigerator-wide torso, Graves had to stand back in the trees to avoid silhouetting himself, even at this distance.

Earlier, he had heard gunshots while inspecting a freshwater spring site near one of his grow sites. When his two men didn't respond on their walkie-talkies, he figured they were in trouble, so he'd trekked up the hill, hoping for a better line of sight to their location.

"We should take out that bitch with the badge and the other dude," said Toko.

"I can drop them both from here," said Ron Petrie, one of McG's senior growers, as he peered through the scope on his Remington 700 rifle.

"If Deputy Monroe weren't there, I'd say go ahead, so stand down." McG zoomed in on the outsider, who had just handed over two AKs to the sheriff. "That guy, though, sure fits the description of the dude Merle told us about. Said he went by Payne."

"You think Payne's DEA?" asked Toko.

"Or an undercover with the state task force," said McG. "But since he spent most of yesterday afternoon in lockup, who knows. Either way, I'll get ahold of my contact in Absynth. I wanna know if heat is gonna come down on us here. Plus, anyone with balls enough to walk into one of my camps without backup and take down two of my guys is someone I need to be concerned about."

He lowered his binoculars and gazed at the forest beyond the creek. "That was a productive forty acres. Now, that loss is going to cut into my bottom line at a time when I can't afford any shortfalls."

Petrie slid back from his rifle. "What about Derek and Nate? They'll get taken over to the jail in Redding after the deputy processes them."

McG moved back from the tree line and headed down the opposite side of the hill towards his Jeep. He kept all of the men working at his numerous grow sites compartmentalized in case they were arrested. Each of them only knew their particular parcel of weed and nothing else about the larger operation. "That's on them. They knew the risks when they signed on. Plus, those guys are gonna have their arms in slings for a while by the looks of it, so they're no longer of any use to me."

CHAPTER 20

Schulz pulled the black Suburban off the interstate south of Sacramento, following the red blip on the GPS, which indicated Eva Daly's location.

"Nearly five hours without a piss break...she's tougher than a two-dollar steak," said Elke from the rear seat.

"She's running scared. Wouldn't you be, too, if you thought something bad had happened to your brother?" replied Wagner.

Elke smirked. "My brother can rot in hell for all I care, if he's not already there."

"Close family, were you?" quipped Schulz.

"At least I had a human family and didn't hatch out of an egg. Besides, if I ever run into my brother, my blade's going into that pedo's gut."

"Violence isn't always the answer," said Simon in a sarcastic tone.

She shrugged her shoulders, gazing out the window. "What else is there?"

"Not everyone deserves to die," Wagner said. "But many will suffer those consequences if they interfere with Bana's operations in any shape or form, and we're on this road trip to ensure that doesn't happen. Whatever is necessary, remember that."

Schulz pulled into a gas station across from the one where Eva was filling up her Toyota RAV4. Regal exited the Suburban, heading to the pump, while Schulz went into the minimart.

"You've been with Bana the longest of any of us...why have you stayed with him all these years?" Elke asked Wagner.

It was a fair question. Bana paid extremely well and treated each of his former GSG operators with respect. Some eventually went on to other lines of work or retired, but Wagner had been with his boss for nine years, rising to the top and overseeing security operations throughout Eastern Europe.

"Because he was like us at one time and came up from the trenches. I served under him briefly in the GSG, so when he called me a few years later, after I'd been doing bullshit security details for celebrities, I jumped at the chance to work with him again. Plus, loyalty is not a company slogan for him. It *is* everything, and it's what separates our group from cutthroat mercenaries and contractors."

Wagner swiveled around to face Elke, resting his hand on her knee. "I know you have only been with Bana for two months, but you should stick around. It'll be worth it on many levels."

She pursed her lips. "And you're not just saying that because we're fucking?"

"That might figure into it, but you will be hard-pressed to find another employer like Mikal Bana."

"So are the stories true...about Bana and his wife wiping out the Orlov family and taking over the old man's business all those years ago? I mean, she was an Orlov herself, and she killed her entire extended family, even the little kids."

Wagner nodded. "Alina is as ruthless as her husband, and she despised her own blood." He turned back around. "But the kids didn't die at her hands...or even Bana's. I was the one who saw to the problem-solving that night."

Elke's mouth hung open. She leaned forward, sliding her hand between his legs. "You'll have to tell me about it some-time. I want to hear every detail."

A moment later, the two men returned. Schulz watched Eva leave and head to the highway, waiting a minute before following her.

"Absynth is only a few thousand people," said Schulz. "The four of us are going to stand out."

Wagner nodded. "We'll have to split into two groups. You and Regal will stay on Eva while Elke and I take care of some other leads." He shot a glance at Regal, who also doubled as their tech expert. "Depending on what unfolds, I may need you to put a blanket over the town so there's a complete blackout of telecoms and internet."

"Shouldn't be a problem."

"We also need to acquire another vehicle before we get there," said Schulz.

Wagner enhanced the map on his tablet, studying the outlying cities. "Redding is a college town an hour from Absynth, so we'll have our pick of beat-up cars."

"Rules of engagement with the locals in Absynth?" said Elke.

Wagner glanced at his team. "The gloves are off. Just find Daly's research and burn through anyone who gets in the way."

CHAPTER 21

"So tell me again how you subdued those two men," said Monroe as she sat at her desk, staring at Payne, who was leaning against the doorframe. "And more importantly, what were you doing in the upper reaches of that creek? That area isn't exactly a tourist attraction."

He had thought about how this might play out since it's not every day a random visitor to the region happens across a backcountry dope-growing operation and lives to talk about it.

The question hung in the air as Monroe steepled her fingers while gazing at him.

Payne moved into the room and sat down across from her. "The dead guy found in his vehicle...you remember, the one you accused me of killing."

She smirked, leaning back.

He continued, "I noticed when you stopped at the crime scene to talk to your forensics guy that the victim had red clay on his boots. Saw it when he was being removed from the vehicle. Found that odd since all the trails I've been on around here are made up of black soil."

"And you just opened a map and figured out that particular creek was filled with red clay. So you're a geologist now?"

"I did better than a map. Talked to Paige at her pottery gallery. You know the one near that earwig motel you recommended after you drove me back to town 'cause my bike was shot to pieces following my arrest."

She blew a strand of blonde hair off her nose. "So glad you're not the type to hold a grudge." Monroe waved a hand. "Go on."

"Paige told me that she gathers her clay from a couple of different riverbeds in the area. And she filled me in on where a few of those are. Out of curiosity, I thought I'd check 'em out."

"I see. First off, I did notice the clay on the deceased's boots when I was downstairs with the coroner yesterday evening. It's in my report and something of interest, but as you may have noticed, we're a bit short on manpower around here, so that was low on my list. Secondly, did it occur to you that you might have just fouled up any evidence in that creek bed by trampling the ground near the clay source?"

"I hear what you're saying, but it's not what you mean. What you meant to say is, 'Thank you, Kyle, for taking down two gun-toting thugs who were growing an illegal crop in my backyard.'"

Her expression became grim. "You think this is all a joke? That your little one-man-army routine with those goons, and with that shoot-out at the campground, means you're a part of my team or something?"

"Deputy Monroe, I clearly hit a sore spot, and it was not my intention. Well, at least not entirely after yesterday morning, but I assure you that there wasn't any indication of human tracks in that creek bed, so it was not the spot where the victim had been. And having worked a lot of cases with my father in the backcountry, I am aware of protecting scene integrity at all costs to preserve evidence."

He must have used the right buzzwords, as her shoulders suddenly relaxed. "You're damn lucky those two idiots didn't snipe you from behind."

"Agreed." He couldn't recount how many times he'd thought such things before on missions abroad. "Those bush hippies said 'McG' was their boss. He's the one you told me about yesterday."

She nodded. "Matt Graves. Been running illegal cannabis operations from Redding to the Oregon border and probably beyond. He's a slippery bastard. He's better equipped than we are, and has a few dozen guys working for him, who are usually Filipinos. He uses drones when he gets word from his scouts that the feds are in the area and then clears out and goes dark for a while. Graves learned the trade from his uncle Amos, who knows every valley, stream and mountain pass around here as well as the surveyors."

Monroe swiveled to the left, pointing to a wall map. "See that area highlighted in red...that's the Emerald Triangle I was talking about before. Nearly every state has such regions, each of them controlled by guys like McG."

"I thought marijuana was legal in California now."

"It is, but ninety percent of the dispensaries still get their grass from illegal growers since it's cheaper than dealing with all the greenhouse permits to produce their own. Plus, guys like Graves sell literally tons of dope in other states that haven't legalized marijuana."

"How come the DEA hasn't shut him down?"

"He's what they call a mid-level player, and he's not a violent felon who's ever killed anyone, that I know of..." Her last few words trailed off as she glanced towards the door in the hallway that led to the morgue.

"In my experience in other countries, law enforcement

often likes to keep a few regional players like him in circulation so they have an ear to the ground. Round up all the drug dealers and you've just lost a considerable source of intelligence."

He left out the part about how the officers were often on the payroll of such drug dealers. He'd already pushed a few too many buttons with Monroe. Plus, he sensed she was a woman of integrity working in a district with too many miles to cover and not enough funding.

Payne glanced at his watch. "Well, if there aren't any further questions about what happened at the creek, then I need to be on my way."

"To another creek bed in search of tracks? I sure hope not."

He stood and pressed a hand to his stomach. "A late lunch, actually."

She got up and followed him to the door. "And after that?"

"Thought I'd check out some of the historic sites in the area, maybe visit that old sawmill east of town."

"And earlier you said you were going to read but instead went snooping around in the backcountry. I'm not kidding about not mucking up any potential spots that could help me with my case. I've got enough on my hands right now."

"I will certainly try to avoid running into any more amateur farmers in the backcountry."

Monroe motioned towards the secretary at the front desk. "Dottie, will you please show Mr. Payne to his car before I take him out back and beat him."

He smirked. "Suddenly, it feels like I'm back in Arizona."

CHAPTER 22

It was just before 9 p.m. when Eva pulled into the Absynth County Sheriff's Department. The long drive north from LA had been a blur, and she had hardly eaten or drank anything except for a deli sandwich at a gas station stop near Sacramento and a blueberry muffin and Coke in Redding.

The only other stop she'd made was at Aaron's small house south of town. The dwelling looked as she remembered it, and nothing seemed out of place. Except she did notice his laptop was missing, along with a tattered but coveted shoulder bag adorned with patches from the different national parks he'd visited.

Now, the only logical solution to locating her brother was waiting in this building. She exited her RAV4 and arched her back in a stretch, trying to relieve the tension in her neck that she was certain was the culprit behind her growing headache.

Eva looked down Main Street, noticing a few new stores and a strip plaza that hadn't been there during her last visit several years ago. She thought about the steak dinner she and Aaron had shared, talking about their respective careers and their futures.

He was always so excited about his work. She felt her headache growing like her skull was the size of a bowling ball. *Where the hell are you, big brother?*

She locked her car and headed in through the front doors. Eva stood before the redheaded woman at the front counter, surprised to see the secretary still at work. "Can I help you, sweetie?"

"I'm here to see Sheriff Hanson."

"He's out. Can I ask what this is about?" the older woman said.

"I'm Eva Daly. I'd like to file a missing person report for my brother, Aaron."

The woman's expression softened. "Oh, my goodness, Eva, I almost didn't recognize you." She started to roll back in her chair and stand, but a deputy appeared around the corner, moving towards the front desk. "I'll take it from here, Dottie, thanks. Why don't you call it a night?"

"Becky, my God, it's so good to see you," Eva said to Monroe.

The deputy smiled as both women leaned in and hugged. "It's been, what, probably five years since you were last up this way."

"Yeah, Derek's wedding," she said with a smile, recalling the marriage of Monroe's brother.

The deputy put her arm around Eva. "Why don't you come into my office so we can talk."

"Alright, sure." Eva reluctantly trudged forward, wanting only to file her report, then head out on the local roads, searching for her brother.

Once in Monroe's office, Eva sat down and found it unusual that her friend closed the door and sat next to her rather than at her desk. "I've been trying to get ahold of Aaron for two days after he left me a cryptic message. I was just at his house, but there's no sign of…"

Monroe rested her hand on top of Eva's. "There's no easy way to tell you this, but we found Aaron's body yesterday morning. He was, um, he was shot several times and was found in his vehicle in the woods not far from the Elkhorn Campground. I'm so sorry, Eva."

She felt like the walls were constricting, and she fought to take a breath. Eva leaned back as the news percolated through her weary brain. "No, that can't be. He can't be dead. Who would want to…" She held a hand to her mouth as tears streamed down her cheeks. "Aaron was the kind of guy everyone loved. Why would someone kill him?"

Eva got up and paced around the room. Her instinct was to bolt for the door and run, and keep running. Monroe had to be wrong. They must have found someone else's body. Someone who resembled Aaron.

"He must be turned around in the forest somewhere, like he always used to be. He'll turn up soon." She balled her fists until the nails bit into her palms. "It can't be him."

Monroe stood and handed her a Kleenex from her desk. "I'm sorry, but it's Aaron. It took a while to ID him. We didn't have your number to even call, or I would have as soon as I found out."

Eva snapped her head at Monroe. "Why did it take a while?"

The deputy lowered her head. "He was shot multiple times in the abdomen, and his face looked like a wild animal or feral dog had gotten to him before we did."

Eva pulled away, walking to the opposite wall and pressing her back against it like it was about to topple upon her. "This doesn't make any sense. He was a bug guy. An entomologist." She gave Monroe a hard stare. "Was it the fucking pot growers? Did he stumble across one of McG's farms or something?"

"I'm not sure. We have a few leads, but the one person

who looked promising yesterday didn't pan out. The state guys and the DEA are providing assistance, but it's just me and a new deputy who are running point on this."

"You already had someone in custody?"

Monroe nodded. "It was the wrong guy. His alibis check out. No way he could have done it based upon the time of death."

"What about Hanson...is he dragging his ass on the investigation? Or did he fall off the wagon again? Is that why he's not here?"

She shook her head. "He's been sober going on six years. He's having some back issues and headed home a few hours ago. Too many rodeos in younger days, so, sometimes, he has to call it quits partway through his shift."

Eva glanced at the door. "Is Aaron..." She paused, pressing her hands against her face. "Is he here?"

Monroe sighed. "Yes. I can take you downstairs, but I should warn you that—"

"I was a war correspondent for years. I'm not afraid of anything you are going to show me."

But she was terrified. Because seeing her brother's bullet-riddled body would mean it was real, and right now she still held out an ounce of hope that she was trapped in a bad dream.

———

SHORTLY AFTER EMERGING from the coroner's room, Monroe found Eva sitting on the back steps of the sheriff's department, cradling a cup of decaf coffee that she'd gotten from the break room.

"You still take it with enough milk to drown a cow," Monroe quipped, settling beside her with her own steaming cup as they both stared out at the forest beyond the parking lot.

Eva's lips quivered. "Some things never change."

"Like you hiding out by the woods when you need to think." Monroe bumped her shoulder gently. "Remember junior year? After Danny Kelham asked us both to prom?"

"God, you sat with me at the park for two hours while I alternated between swearing and sobbing." Eva shook her head. "You were the only one who knew I had a crush on him too."

"And then neither of us went with him because…"

"Sisters before misters," they finished in unison, sharing a tired laugh.

The levity faded as Eva stared into her cup. "I should have been around for you, Beck. After Derek…"

"Hey, it's OK." Monroe's voice was firm but gentle. "Aaron told me you were heading overseas for work and to relay your condolences. I got your message before the funeral about having to head overseas for work. I get it. You were living your life."

"Still. There were phone calls I could have made; visits back here I kept putting off." She swallowed hard. "And now Aaron…"

Monroe set down her coffee and gripped Eva's hand. "You and I are going to work through this. That's what matters." She glanced up at the sky. "Both of our brothers are probably laughing about you being here, given how much you tried to convince them that Absynth was just a one-horse town that you couldn't wait to get out of."

"Trust me, it really is," said Eva.

They both chuckled, then sat in silence, watching a sliver of moonlight pierce the clouds over the mountains while both women became lost in their thoughts.

CHAPTER 23

AFTER A MORNING RUN, PAYNE SHOWERED AND EXITED HIS motel room, walking across the street to the sheriff's department. He wanted to check on what happened with the two dope growers he had encountered at the creek, and if there was any word on whether Merle had been apprehended. It would help him sleep a little easier knowing the meth-head wasn't lurking in the shadows with another hit crew.

He entered the lobby of the building and went to the front desk, exchanging pleasantries with Dottie, who thankfully acted like she'd forgotten he had occupied the corner cell a couple of days ago.

"Deputy Monroe will be with you shortly," she said, then motioned towards the four chairs in the right corner, where a woman was waiting.

He walked over and sat down, both of them nodding at one another. Payne could see her eyes were red and puffy. Despite that, her hands and face were tanned, though she didn't have the well-worn fingernails of someone used to manual labor in the outdoors.

Reaching over to pick up a fishing magazine off the small

table between them, he paused to glance along her neck. "Excuse me," he said, pointing to her wooden pendant. "Is that Aja, by chance?"

She lifted a hand, holding up the flat disk, which held the carved image of a woman with long hair. "Surprised to hear someone know that in Absynth of all places."

"I'm not from here, but I've spent some time in Kenya and recall how important that goddess is to the native cultures there."

She gazed at his scruffy beard and shaggy hair tucked under his ball cap. "You don't seem like a tourist."

"Sort of." He saw Dottie giving him an embarrassed glance. "Just passing through on a road trip."

She pointed at his boots. "I was wondering if you were a PCT hiker...Pacific Crest Trail. It's not far from here."

"Trekking over two thousand miles isn't my idea of fun."

She stroked the pendant. "All these years, I've never had anyone recognize this image in the States. I spent a few months in Africa two years ago, covering gemstone mining and how it's impacting the indigenous people along the border of Ethiopia and Kenya." She gazed over his face again. "Were you in the Peace Corps over there?"

He held back a chuckle since peace had never been an element during his missions in Africa. "Business, actually. I used to do consulting for several companies overseas."

Monroe came around the corner and froze in her tracks, staring at the two of them. "Wait, do you guys know each other?"

They shook their heads in unison before standing.

Monroe seemed relieved. She waved a hand at the woman. "Eva, this is Kyle Payne, and Kyle, this is Eva Daly."

As an awkward cloud hung in the air between him and the deputy, Payne filled in the thought bubble over Monroe's head. *And Kyle was the number one suspect in your brother's murder.*

Payne extended a hand towards Eva. "My condolences on your loss."

The woman gave him a puzzled look that held an underlying plea behind her eyes. "Did you know my brother?"

"No, I've just heard a lot about him from the deputy."

"Unless it's something urgent, maybe we can talk later?" Monroe said to Payne with a "leave now" expression.

"Nice to meet you," said Payne as he glanced at Eva on his way out. Though he wished it were under different circumstances for both of them.

———

PAYNE HEADED to the west side of Absynth, stopping at the mechanic's to check on the status of his bike. The man informed him that he had a half-dozen vehicles ahead of Payne. Plus, it was going to be at least three more days until the parts for the bike were shipped up from an Indian Motorcycle dealer in LA.

He decided to use his time to get settled in at the field station since Tommy Larkin had texted him the code for the lockbox on the main gate of the property.

The drive out to the site took thirty minutes on the graded dirt road, and almost every bend on the scenic route overlooked a stunning meadow or sweeping view of the mountains. He could see why the region had been chosen for the Sycamore Creek field station, which hosted classes on wildlife biology, ethnobotany, ornithology and animal tracking.

After eleven miles, he came to a halt, pausing to step out and unlock the wrought-iron gate that stretched across the road. The smell of spruce and pine permeated the moist air, and he sucked in a lungful, feeling some of the tension in his shoulders drain away from the past few days of chaos.

Payne drove along the meandering road for another mile, then up an incline towards a cluster of log-cabin-style structures peppering the hillside. He parked next to a large propane tank beside the dining hall and got out, surveying his new surroundings.

From what he recalled from the online description, the place was administered by a consortium of community colleges and universities who utilized the 290-acre site for educational and research opportunities. During the hot, dry months of early summer, it was often used as an incident command post and staging site for fire-suppression units that coordinated with the nearby lookout towers.

Two perennial streams flowed through the property, and the site was surrounded by thousands of acres of untrammeled wilderness. Payne leaned against the Subaru, feasting his eyes upon his surroundings, which helped to partially wash away the unpleasant residue of his time in Absynth.

He grabbed his pack from the back seat and headed up the gravel path that led to the student cabins. Along the way, he paused to glance in the windows of the six other structures, which looked like they were used as either classrooms or research facilities, along with a generator shack, bathhouse, and a caretaker's cabin. Larkin had indicated the latter individual was gone for a few days, so Payne would have the property to himself.

Despite the old log structures seeming like they belonged to the nineteenth century, each one contained a numeric security keypad on the doors. He glanced at the text again from Larkin and entered the code for the last cabin.

Stepping inside the ten-by-twenty abode, he was greeted by the aroma of bug spray mingled with Pine-Sol. The place held two sets of bunkbeds, a table with two chairs, and a coat rack in the corner beside one of two windows.

During his many years with the CIA, he'd slept in caves, boulder fields, jungles, snow trenches and military barracks the world over, so this tiny cabin seemed like the lap of luxury.

And a far cry from my hammock.

He dropped his pack on one of the bunks and headed outside, walking back to the rental car to get his food. Payne went into the dining hall, placing his goods in the walk-in fridge and the pantry.

Returning to the parking lot, he observed the distance of the sun to the treetops across the valley.

Three hours of light left. Just enough time to do some exploring.

Only he wasn't interested in reconnoitering his immediate surroundings. He'd seen another outcropping of red clay beside a stream during the drive in. One that Paige had failed to mention.

It bothered Payne immensely that Hanson had so easily assumed he was behind Daly's murder due to an anonymous call. It seemed like shoddy investigative work, and Payne wondered if the old sheriff would still try to find some means of connecting him to the killing.

Not if I have anything to say in the matter. If Hanson isn't going to do a thorough job, then I'll have to do my own investigation. No way I'm gonna get tossed back in that cell because of that lazy ass.

Payne made sure he had a full water bottle and his folding knife, then got into the Subaru, retracing his route back through the forested valley.

CHAPTER 24

Sheriff Hanson finished feeding his horses and returned to the back porch of his house, pausing to lean against the railing. Even though he had only been working for a half hour, his back and hips were already aching. Another reason why he had slowly been turning over his responsibilities to Monroe and why his office hours had been reduced this fall. If he could just make it a few more months to March, he could retire with a full thirty years under his belt.

Hanson pulled a pack of Marlboros from his shirt pocket and lit one up, taking a long drag and staring at his three horses in the meadow, then up towards Pittman Mountain in the distance. With his two kids grown and living out of state, and his wife having died six years ago, he wondered how much longer he could manage his twenty-acre property on the outskirts of town.

Hanson heard the gravel crunching in the driveway around the front and wondered who was coming out to visit on his day off. He stabbed out the cigarette and tossed it in an empty coffee can near the steps and walked along the sandstone pathway to the drive.

"Good afternoon, Sheriff," a man in a black blazer said with a slight accent as he stepped out of a black Suburban while a woman with short blonde hair did the same. They both flashed bronze badges but not long enough for Hanson to make out much.

"I'm Agent Mike Sanville, and this is Agent Margaret Bleeker. We're with the USDA, investigating the death of one of our contract workers, Aaron Daly."

"And you decided to come to my house. How the hell did you even find me, anyway?"

The man thrust his thumb over his shoulder. "Stopped in at your office, and they said you were at home today. I hope you don't mind if we ask you a few questions?"

Hanson didn't like how close the two had gotten, and he took a step back, resting a hand on his back pocket, where he had a Ruger snubbie .22 Magnum that he carried for rattlesnakes. "How about you come to my office tomorrow when I'm back at work. We can talk then. And that's not a question, by the way."

The woman walked to the right a few feet, standing beside Hanson's yellow tractor. It made him further edgy since his attention was now split between the two locations.

"We'd just like to know if you uncovered anything on Aaron Daly's research. We believe that's what may have gotten him killed," said the man. Hanson was sure he detected a slight German accent.

"You figure that's what killed him, eh? You guys at the USDA must have some fuckin' rocket scientists on staff to put that together when we only just ID'd Daly's body two days ago."

"We have an elite team for sure," the man said. "But did you learn anything about Daly's research lab? We were told he had one around these parts."

"Don't know anything about that, but like I said, very

politely, the first time, we can talk more tomorrow, or you can go to the department and speak with my deputy."

"No, I don't think our assignment can wait, Sheriff. We have quite a pressing timeline."

The woman took a few more steps, arcing out to Hanson's right.

If he was going to pull out his pistol, now was the time to do it while he could still control the scene.

As if sensing his thoughts, the man moved slowly towards the front porch. Now, the two arrivals were at ten and two, making it impossible to cover them both.

Shit. What the hell is happening here? He had a sinking feeling in his gut, chiding himself for losing the tactical advantage. "You both need to get back in your vehicle and leave before you really piss me off."

"But you haven't answered my question, Jerry. May I call you Jerry...or is it Gerald?" He glanced across at the woman. "I think Gerald sounds more like a banker than a sheriff."

"Agree. Jerry seems much more appropriate for a gully-jumper like this one. He's also older than I thought he'd be. His photo online must be twenty years younger."

Hanson slid his hand onto his pistol. Then he felt his left knee explode with pain, the suppressed gunshot only striking his ears after he collapsed to the ground, holding his shattered kneecap. He felt bile rushing up in this throat and vomited as he rolled onto his side.

The man in the black blazer moved in closer, his hands empty. He pressed his boot onto the sheriff's chest. "Tell me everything about Aaron Daly and I promise I won't drag this out."

"Fuck you," shouted Hanson. He tried to move on his side and reach the pistol in his pocket, but the man slammed his boot down on his right hand, snapping the fingers. Hanson shrieked, coiling into a fetal position. "I'm gonna hang your ass from a tree out back, boy."

"That's the spirit, Sheriff. My respect for old lawmen like you would have plummeted if you had just caved in to my demands."

The man removed the pistol from Hanson's back pocket, glancing at the cylinder. "A .22 Magnum. This round can sure do a helluva lot of damage, even for a small caliber." He handed it to the woman, then grabbed Hanson's shirt collar and dragged him across the gravel to the tractor. He leaned him against the front tire and slid off Hanson's leather belt, securing his good hand to the metal footstep.

The man moved aside a few feet and motioned to his partner, who moved up in front of the sheriff. "Let's see what that little pistol can do…just spare the vitals for now. I need him conscious."

"I've got enough hearing loss." She slid the .22 in her jacket and removed a folding blade, kneeling beside Hanson and deftly slicing through the muscles on his forearm.

The man waited a few minutes until Hanson's squeals had diminished before leaning over him. "If I were you, Sheriff, I'd start talking. Her father was a butcher in the old country, and she knows how to use a blade like few others."

CHAPTER 25

AFTER VISITING WITH MONROE TO SEE IF THERE WERE ANY MORE leads on her brother's murder, Eva returned to Aaron's house.

She had no idea how much time had passed as she sat at the dining room table, sifting through his calendar book and sticky notes on the fridge for the twentieth time. There was nothing here that was going to provide a clue to his final days or hours.

What did you discover about that invasive beetle species, Aaron?

She wasn't surprised that Monroe thought Aaron's death was connected with him stumbling across some dope-grower's site.

Except she knew Aaron's cryptic text message involved something he'd discovered at the Wayland agricultural facility outside of Absynth. When Aaron had first called her last week while she was on assignment for her newspaper in Istanbul, he indicated that he'd discovered an unusual beetle that was only endemic to Europe.

She recalled the urgency in his voice on the last night they spoke. *If I'm right about this, then Wayland could be involved in something that will have global ramifications for the agricultural industry throughout Europe. And it will have all begun right here in our own backyard. I just need to locate an insect specimen to send it down to Gabe for further analysis. I'll know more soon, but I don't want to sound crazy or like some conspiracist until I can prove my theory.*

She replayed the words in her mind, hearing his voice as if he were sitting across from her. She wanted to reach out and hold his hand, just one more time. Eva felt a wave of tears coming and leaned her head down while sobbing.

A few minutes later, after the tsunami of anguish had passed, she stared ahead. Then she remembered something unusual about one of Monroe's comments down in the coroner's room. Eva's eyes darted along the tiled floor as she reflected on the red clay that had been caked on her brother's boots.

She shot up, grabbing her shoulder bag and heading for the front door, knowing exactly where her brother's final moments had been spent.

———

THEO DAVENPORT SLID OPEN the drawer in his teak desk, pulling out a bottle of Tums. He popped two in his mouth and stood, moving to the large bay windows overlooking his company's courtyard, five stories below.

He watched several employees sitting at the picnic tables, enjoying their lunches and taking turns glancing at something on their phones while laughing.

Davenport could barely recall such carefree days. He had lived a life of servitude to this place, beginning in high school and since he took over his father's corporation twenty-two years ago just after turning forty.

Through Theo's innovative business strategies, he had expanded what had once been a regional wheat distribution chain to a nationwide enterprise where his corporation controlled the supply of the grain industry in the US.

Despite having numerous estates around the world and whatever worldly pleasures he desired, it had never been enough. Manipulating the fates of others around him had always served as his motivating force, and now, with the coming delivery of the weaponized pathogen that Bana would disseminate throughout Europe, Davenport would be able to control the fate of entire nations.

He removed his iPhone, calling his small agro-facility outside of Absynth.

His head of security, Anton Fischer, answered on the first ring as expected. "How may I be of service, sir?"

"Anything further on locating Daly's research?"

"Nothing, sir. We've combed through his house but don't have any other leads. And Graves said there wasn't anything in Daly's vehicle."

"What about a girlfriend or buddy of his?"

"He grew up here, so he knew everyone, sir, but there doesn't appear to be one person in particular who stood out as being closer to him than others."

Davenport felt the acid in his stomach surging up in his throat again. He wanted to reach through the phone and crush the life out of the man on the other end. "Be advised that a colleague of mine involved in the hunt for Daly's files has his own people in Absynth now. You will provide any assistance they request, if asked."

"But my team and I know the area and are—"

"Any assistance, is that clear? These are some heavy hitters, so don't piss them off or get in the way. Just do what they ask."

"Yes, of course, sir. Should I involve Graves and his men?" said Fischer.

"No, not yet. They're nothing more than apes with clubs at this point, keeping an eye on the immediate woods around our place."

"That's a relief, actually. I don't trust the man."

"His trust is ensured for now with what I'm paying him."

"Are you still expecting to arrive here on Sunday morning to obtain the pathogen?"

"Unless there's some drastic change in the weather, I'll be there. My helicopter pilot has flown in far worse, so nothing is going to stand in my way." Davenport didn't wait for a response and signed off.

He thought about calling Bana to assure him of the time-line. The oligarch had his own pressing window for delivering the weaponized insect pathogen since the narrow window for unleashing the vermin would be closing by month's end.

Plus, he didn't want to aggravate Bana since he'd already asked his man Wagner to tie off all the loose ends in Absynth by eliminating Graves along with all of the staff at the Wayland research facility following the Sunday pickup.

Davenport gazed at the gray cumulus clouds stacking up along the horizon, confident that the only good thing about the coming storm was that it would wash away all the blood that was about to be spilled in Absynth.

CHAPTER 26

PAYNE DROVE HIS RENTAL CAR BACK ALONG THE DIRT ROAD HE came in on until he arrived at the two-lane blacktop. He crossed, making a dogleg to the other side and onto a narrow dirt road that dead-ended a hundred yards beyond.

After getting out and grabbing his daypack, he headed down the short slope that led to the creek bed. With the incredibly shallow water that was flowing through the drainage, he was starting to get the feeling that anything labeled as a river by the locals was little more than a stream.

He crossed several flat rocks, making it to the other side and proceeding in the opposite direction from the road. After only a few minutes of walking in the forest, he saw it. The same sliver of clay he'd seen from the road. Only this was a long band of red substrate that extended fifty yards along the creek. Payne knelt, examining some of the raccoon, deer and fox tracks but not seeing any signs of Daly's boot prints.

Getting up, he continued walking along the shoreline. Twenty feet ahead, his eyes zoomed in on a string of human tracks. His pace quickened.

He scrutinized the first print, which showed a perfectly preserved Vibram boot sole identical to what Aaron Daly had been wearing.

Payne walked a parallel path to the tracks, noting the stride and straddle of the maker. From what he recalled working man-tracking cases with his father, he knew that the stride measured the distance from one heel to the next. This could be used to roughly determine the average walking speed of a person, and the stride before him was in accordance with what a guy Aaron Daly's height would have made.

Payne removed his phone and snapped off a few dozen photos from different angles and under different kinds of light conditions, using his body to create shadows for contrast.

He climbed up out of the stream bed and glanced down at Daly's manuscript of movement in the clay.

But why was he here?

Payne followed a game trail that skirted along the creek, eventually coming to a transition zone where the forest met a field. A few feet beyond the trees was an eight-foot-high fence rimmed with razor wire.

His eyes traced the perimeter of the fence line, which extended well beyond his vision to the south, but only thirty feet to a corner post on his right.

Beyond the fence were what appeared to be hundreds of acres of some kind of crop that resembled wheat or alfalfa. Beyond that was a large, two-story structure with an odd blend of old and new architecture. The front appeared to be a Victorian-style house with wooden upright beams between a large porch and an upstairs veranda, while the back of the building looked like a modern steel warehouse had been lowered in place.

Payne took a few steps forward, grabbing a piece of dried

plant stalk that was sticking out through the fence. He yanked it free and turned it over in his hand, certain that it was wheat.

He walked down to the nearest corner of the fence, reading the yellow metal sign fixed to the chain-link.

Private Property of Wayland Corporation
No Trespassing
No Hunting
No Biologists or Botanists

Payne snapped off another photo. *Never seen a warning that specific before.* He glanced back at the creek bed, imagining Daly doing fieldwork and then coming here. *Did Daly find something that pissed off someone at Wayland? Doesn't seem like that would lead to his death.*

He spun around at the sound of a cracking branch.

A figure emerged from the creek. The woman walking towards him was Eva Daly. She suddenly froze, jutting her face up from the trail at him. "You again?"

"Did you follow me?" he asked.

"No. What the hell are you doing here?"

"I could ask you the same thing." But he already knew the answer.

———

ANTON FISCHER HAD JUST SAT down at his computer monitor to have lunch when he noticed one of Wayland's security consoles light up. He paused mid-bite, setting down his sandwich and scrutinizing the video feed from one of the remote cameras set up along the southeastern perimeter of the eighty-acre agricultural facility.

"Who the hell are these people?" He felt his pulse quicken

at the thought of another intruder on their property after what had happened to Aaron Daly a few days ago.

He grabbed the walkie-talkie off the desk. "Teams one and two, get over to the fence line by perimeter 4A now! We've got unwanted visitors. They need to be removed from the site before they get any further."

————

EVA SHOT a piercing gaze at Payne. "You said you didn't know my brother, but I think you did…or you know what he was doing out here. Were you working with him?"

"No, I just thought I came across something connected with his murder."

"But you said you were just visiting the area. Are you a private investigator? Is that why you came to see Monroe?"

This was getting more complicated by the minute. He didn't know how to explain his actions, and revealing he had been a chief murder suspect was only going to cause her to panic.

Before he could formulate his next sentence, sirens began blaring beyond the fence line.

"Shit, we need to go." He ran by her, pausing to grab her wrist. "Now!"

They trotted down into the creek bed, retracing their paths along the shoreline, ducking under branches and trying to stay upright on the slick clay in a mad dash for their vehicles.

Coming to the grassy slope he'd first taken after arriving, Payne peered above the edge. "Looks clear by our cars. Let's meet in town at that coffee shop, and I can tell you why I was here."

"Deal."

They sprang up and ran for the parking area, a hundred

yards away. Payne only got halfway when he saw two guys rush from the trees.

From their body odor and barefoot appearance, they looked more like McG's bush hippies. The first one slammed directly into Payne's side in a linebacker tackle, driving him to the ground. The larger one at the rear grabbed Payne's ankles, but that only resulted in a swift kick to the guy's chin, which sent him reeling back into a tree.

The guy on top of Payne began straddling his chest. Payne grabbed the man's shirt collar and yanked his torso down while sending a straight punch into his throat. The guy gasped, grabbing his windpipe, and Payne thrust his own hips up and to the right, bucking the attacker up enough to slide out.

Someone else enveloped Payne's entire chest and arms in a bear hug from behind.

These guys just keep coming like fire ants.

He leaned his head forward, then slammed it back hard in a vicious head butt that he felt connect. The attacker groaned, loosening his grip slightly but not enough to free Payne's arms, so he leaned forward again, but deeper this time until he felt the weight of his attacker on his hips. Payne swiveled his body hard to the right and let gravity do the rest. This guy tumbled onto his back with all of Payne's weight on top of him.

Payne hopped up and sent his boot into the guy's head, knocking him out cold. He reached down for the Glock in the man's beltline but was startled at the sound of gunfire.

"That's enough," shouted a voice behind him.

He turned and saw an immense man with a black goatee clutching Eva's arm, while three men in security guard uniforms pointed their AR rifles at Payne.

"Matt Graves, what a surprise," said Eva in a sarcastic tone.

Graves glanced at her face as his mouth hung open. "Damn, Eva, I thought you had brains enough to stay away from this town for good." He motioned towards his men. "Tie 'em up and toss them in the back of my van. I'll handle the rest."

CHAPTER 27

WHILE IT HAD ONLY BEEN A THIRTY-MINUTE DRIVE IN THE BACK of Graves' 4x4 van, the bumpy road made Payne think they were being churned inside a cement truck.

The vehicle looked to be an older model, and from the wood debris and pieces of dead bark scattered along the gutted interior, it was evidently used for transporting lumber and firewood.

All Payne could see beyond Graves and the other thug in the passenger's seat was an endless sea of trees on either side of the road. He figured since neither he nor Eva were blind-folded that operational security wasn't a concern, which told Payne that their abductors planned on this being a one-way trip.

"Keep an eye out for familiar landmarks," he said to Eva as they both tested their rope-bound wrists, which were secured with zip ties to the metal girders along the wall beside them. "We're going to have to make a run for it if an opportunity presents itself." His right hand felt some-thing slender and metallic along the floor by his back pocket. He rolled his thumb and finger, making out the shape of a long wood screw. He inverted his hand, rubbing the coarse spiral edges along the manila rope securing his wrists.

Payne knew it was light-years from a quick solution, but there were few other options.

"You gonna tell me who the hell you are and why you were at Wayland's?" asked Eva.

"Yeah, later, at the coffee shop."

The van slowed, then came to a sudden halt. Payne was sure he heard the sound of chickens clucking outside. He craned his head toward the rear windows, seeing a large meadow and a two-story house with a wraparound porch at the other end. Beyond that was a lone mountain, and he wondered if it was the same one he'd seen to the west of the field station.

Pittman Mountain?

The double doors at the back were yanked open along with the sliding door on the side, followed by four armed men facing Eva and Payne.

Graves barked orders at his men to move the new arrivals into the barn. The Wayland guards were nowhere in sight, and Payne figured they had been taken to one of Graves' remote properties.

A lanky man with missing front teeth climbed inside and used his Leatherman to snip free the zip ties fastening the rope to the metal side paneling.

Payne balled the screw in his fist, pulling his head to the side as the piercing body odor of the thug nearly caused him to gag.

"Get out," the guy said as he retreated through the side door.

Payne and Eva were barely on the ground when they were yanked up to their feet and marched towards an immense barn bordering the woods. The red paint had flaked off long ago, leaving crimson streaks in the grooves of the gray boards.

As they walked, a Rottweiler trotted up, inspecting the visitors, then leaving abruptly, cutting a path through dozens of chickens milling between the ATVs parked beside the barn.

The large double doors were wide open, and Payne saw a handful of men inside, hoisting bunches of recently cut cannabis into the ceiling rafters, where another man was on a plank walkway, spacing out the new product between hundreds of bundles in different stages of drying. When he finished, he descended a wooden ladder built into the wall.

The rest of the sixty-foot-long interior was filled with hay bales, drums of fertilizer, water barrels, several tool benches, and a communal sleeping area at the back, where a dozen cots were lined up beside two folding tables with a camp stove, coffee mugs and an old refrigerator.

They were taken to the right corner and forced to sit on the bare ground. The toothless guy tethered their rope restraints with zip ties against an upright wooden beam. The pillar was sunk into the dirt floor and extended all the way to a horizontal cross-member in the ceiling.

Graves motioned for the four armed men to return to bailing the newly harvested cannabis while he stood before Payne and Eva, swigging down a cup of steaming coffee from a thermos he'd retrieved from the dining area.

"I remember we were in gym class together in tenth grade," said Graves as his eyes traced along Eva's hips and up to her face. "You look as fine as you did then."

She smirked, glancing up at the bundles of dope in the rafters. "Guess the apple really doesn't fall far from the tree. Your uncle Amos must be proud of what you've done with his business."

Graves waved a hand towards the interior. "This is nothing. Wait until harvest time." He stepped closer to Payne.

"Except this asshole cost me a chunk of change recently, along with two of my guys."

"Doesn't your insurance company cover losses like that?" said Payne, who was busy working the screw along his manila restraints.

Graves kicked him in the ribs. "Not sure who the hell you are, but you've been a royal pain in my ass since showing up here a few days ago." The dope dealer put two fingers up to his lips and whistled before waving over a guy who'd just returned from the latrine outside.

Payne stopped abrading the rope around his wrists and stared at Merle's disheveled figure as the man sauntered over.

"Holy shit on a cracker," muttered Merle. "Guess Christmas has come early for me this year."

The meth-head picked a Coke bottle off the table and was about to slam it down on Payne's head when Graves intercepted his arm. "The hell you doing? I called you in here to confirm this is the same guy you dealt with at that campground, not to split his skull open."

"Yeah, it's him alright," Merle replied with a deflated look.

"No shit. I got that when you first walked through the door."

"I think your star employee missed the video on personal hygiene," said Payne, who was nodding down at a piece of toilet paper stuck to the guy's left boot.

"Hey, fuck you, man," snapped Merle as he kicked dirt at Payne's chest.

Graves pressed his bearlike hand against Merle's chest. "Enough, go find Toko and tell 'im I need him in here."

Merle backed up slowly, patting his dainty chest with a fist. "You and me ain't done yet, bro."

Graves glanced down at Payne. "So you took down all of Merle's guys. You undercover DEA or ATF?"

"Just passing through, or so I thought, until Merle's guys shot up my bike the other day, stranding me in this cosmopolitan region."

Graves poured himself another cup of coffee and stared into the contents like it was a divining device. "I couldn't find anything about you in a deep search online or on the dark web. Usually that means someone is working outside of the law or has something shady to hide. My guess is it's the latter, but what would that be, Kyle Payne?"

Payne continued sawing on the rope, feeling some miniscule headway. "Gambling debts...I bet way too much on my nephew's micro-soccer game last month."

Graves sent his boot into Payne's ribs again. He gasped, dropping the screw. "You know what I think...I think maybe you work with one of the outfits up in southern Oregon and were sent down here to scout out my network and try to infiltrate my base of operations."

Payne frantically searched the ground with the limited range of his fingers, but the screw was gone. He paused his activity when Toko entered the barn.

"What the hell happened to you, Matt?" asked Eva. "I always remember you having a tough side, but you were never cruel or a dick, like this."

Graves shuffled back, a surprised look washing over his face for a moment. "People change, Eva. Not all of us had the luxury of working for the family newspaper in Redding and getting a college scholarship. Busting my ass and slowly cornering my uncle's competitors was the only way to get ahead." He stabbed his thumb into his chest. "That's how I took care of my family."

"Does that include killing off other people's family members, like Aaron?" she asked.

Graves tossed his thermos on a hay bale. "Aaron dug his own hole in the ground by fucking around at Wayland's property. This is on him." He lowered his head for a moment. "I mean was."

"How are you even connected to that company? They grow wheat, for God's sake," said Eva.

The dope dealer shook his head, watching as Toko came in. "It's a long story, believe me."

Payne needed to shift his hips to search the ground behind his left hip and needed Graves distracted. "So Wayland's guys killed Aaron Daly and then disfigured his face to slow down the sheriff's investigation, but why park Aaron's vehicle in such an obvious place by the campground? Why not just stash his body in the woods?"

"Because someone prominent like Aaron Daly goes missing in the forest and hundreds of searchers with their dogs and helicopters would be scouring the mountains for him."

"And that would risk your grow sites being discovered," Payne said, finally locating the screw. He nodded at the Glock 17 tucked into Grave's beltline. "Only Aaron was killed by three 9mm hollow points. The Wayland security guys were all carrying HK45s. Totally different ballistics."

Eva's cheeks grew taut. "You killed my brother? For them?" She tried to squirm free, trying to kick him, but Graves stepped aside. "Aaron discovered something Wayland was doing at their research facility, and you killed him for it?"

Graves rubbed the back of his thick neck. "Eva, it didn't go down like that. Well, not initially. My crew were paid a good amount by Wayland to provide security in the woods around their place. In exchange, their soil scientist helped me increase my productivity through the use of their fertilizers. The whole deal was going to be a game-changer for me. Then, a few days ago, we got notified by the Wayland staff that someone was sneaking around the property, and when my guys on the west side of the facility investigated, it turned into a foot chase, with Aaron bolting."

"So you just shot him down like a dog? Did you know what he was doing there in the first place?"

McG leaned a meaty hand against the beam. "To be honest, I didn't even know it was him. I simply got word that an intruder was heading my way, and I shot the first person who stepped out of the woods once I'd confirmed it wasn't one of my own."

"Three times. You really wanted to make sure he was dead," she said as tears welled up in her eyes.

"I didn't make out his face until after I dropped him."

"Would it have even mattered if you knew it was Aaron?"

There was a long pause, then McG replied, "No. My job was to secure Wayland's ops, and he was declared a high-value threat…their words on the radio. And any direct threat to Wayland is an indirect threat to me and my business."

Payne thrust his chin at the bales of dope in the barn. "And you'd do anything to secure your ops here, no matter what the cost? Wayland must have you wedged pretty deep in their back pocket."

McG bent down, grabbing Payne by the shirt collar. "This isn't an op here, it's a family business, asshole. And, yeah, I'd do anything to protect my own blood and everyone who's loyal to me."

The phone buzzed in Graves' vest pocket. He pulled it out, a worried expression seeping over his round face. He answered, then turned and trotted through the side door, yelling back at Toko to watch over things while Graves went back to his house.

Merle immediately walked over and moved up beside Payne, squatting down next to him. The meth-head grabbed the Coke bottle and screwed off the top, taking a long sip. He paused, then swished the soda around and spit it on Payne's leg. "You aren't thirsty, are ya?" said Merle.

Payne slid his body over, using the commotion to vigorously saw through the remaining strands of manila rope. "Just for some new company. Preferably someone with deodorant."

Toko chuckled. The Filipino waved over one of the three men from the workbench against the far wall. "I gotta take a dump. Keep an eye on these two and Merle. Make sure he behaves himself until I find out what the boss wants to do with them."

The gangly figure with the missing upper teeth sat down on a hay bale, pulling out a tin of chewing tobacco and pressing it beneath his lower lip.

Merle slid closer to Payne. "Not so tough, are you now, bird lover; it must suck having your wings clipped."

Payne intentionally whispered something to the man, causing him to lean in closer while he freed his wrists from his bonds. When he was bad-breath distance, Payne scrunched his hips down and swung his right knee up into Merle's face. The vicious blow sent the goon's head into the post above Payne. The goon slumped to the ground like a wet rag.

Payne slid forward, grabbing the Coke bottle and rushing at the thin man hopping up from the bale. Payne connected with the thug's right cheek, then arced it back, sending a crushing blow into the man's trachea. Payne yanked out the Glock 17 from the man's beltline and spun around, using the gasping figure as a shield while he squeezed off a burst of rounds into the two men sprinting towards him from the workbench. He peppered their torsos with hollow points that dropped them in the middle of the barn.

Payne shoved his human shield to the ground, driving his boot heel onto the back of the man's neck and snapping the cervical region. He retrieved a folding knife from the dead guy's pocket and cut Eva loose.

"Somehow, I don't think you're an undercover cop," she said, glancing at the four bodies.

He grabbed her arm and motioned to the rear doors near the workbench. "Let's get to those ATVs. Looked like the keys were in 'em, but first we need to create a distraction that will slow any pursuers."

Payne trotted to the corner, grabbing two gallon jugs of gasoline on the ground. He handed her one and began pouring his container all over the recently baled bundles of pot. "This should do the job."

When they were done, they headed towards the rear doors.

Eva said, "I think we're in Pittman Valley. I recognized the mountain to the north when they were dragging us in here. Follow me when we...look out," Eva shouted as a blur of movement appeared above them.

Toko sprang over a stack of bales, landing in front of Payne. The Filipino sent a stomp kick into Payne's chest that felt like it had crushed his sternum.

Payne landed hard on his back, the Glock disappearing into the bales. Toko leapt at him with a flying sidekick that Payne barely averted. He rolled to his left, coming up into a boxer's stance with the folding knife in his lead hand.

Toko removed a ten-inch fixed blade from his belt, then a smaller curved blade from his other side. The man moved the weapons in a dizzying display of prowess that gave Payne reason to worry. He was no stranger to knife combatives, but his moves were simple compared to the wizardry he was observing.

He would need an equalizer beyond just his folding knife. But there was no time. Toko sprang forward, thrusting the larger blade at Payne's midsection while flicking the tip of the smaller blade at his weapon hand. Payne dodged the first attack, but the second strike nicked him on the shoulder.

He responded by immediately darting at the Filipino, feigning a highline attack at the face, then dropping slightly at the last second and catching Toko on the right quadriceps. It wasn't enough to drastically alter his mobility, but it made the man's grin fade as he backed up, inspecting the wound.

"You have some skill with a blade," said the man.

"Likewise, far more than me, but that won't change the fact that I'm going to kill you." The whole time they had been dueling, Eva had crept to the workbench, grabbing a propane torch. Payne was waiting until his attacker's back was to her before he waved her into action.

She flung the lit torch onto the gasoline-soaked bales; the conflagration was immediate.

Toko swung his head at the burning pile to his right as the flames shot out at his arm.

Payne rushed in, thrusting into the man's abdomen, then darting back out.

The blade fighter staggered back, the flames licking up the back of his cotton T-shirt as he dropped his weapons and fell to his knees.

Payne shuffled to his right, grabbing the Glock and squeezing off a single headshot. He swung around, racing for the bay doors, where Eva was already heading towards the ATVs.

She hopped on the nearest vehicle, starting the engine and taking off. Payne mimicked her actions, throttling another ATV and speeding down the road as flames swept through the entire barn.

A few minutes later, the exploding fuel barrels in the structure sent a shock wave through the forest. They paused at the first trail on the left, watching the smoky-orange cloud billowing up above the meadow.

CHAPTER 28

AFTER THIRTY MINUTES OF DRIVING ALONG THE WINDING GAME trail that led around the base of the mountain, Eva slowed to a stop while Payne pulled up alongside her. Eva's red cheeks were sprinkled with mud droplets, and her arms were trembling.

They turned off their engines and remained still, listening to the forest around them for signs of pursuers. Payne leaned back and searched the storage compartment behind the seat, removing a small first-aid kit. He pulled out an alcohol wipe and a large gauze bandage, cleaning up and dressing the small blade wound on his shoulder.

A short time later, Eva spoke. "That son of a bitch Graves is going to pay."

Payne glanced at the faint wisp of smoke over the treetops to the northwest. "He just lost a chunk of his income, so he's paying alright. Besides, we can't be sure we lost them. He's probably got trail cams and drones at his disposal, so watch your surroundings."

Eva swiveled in her seat to face him, narrowing her eyes.

"Graves mentioned you had gotten into a skirmish with that crack-head at the campground."

"Is that a question?" he inquired.

"Monroe said Sheriff Hanson received a call the morning Aaron's body was discovered, about some guy running from the crime scene back in the direction of Elkhorn Campground."

He nodded. "Yeah, Monroe and her attack poodle arrested me and booked me into their jail, where I enjoyed wasting away an entire day for something I couldn't have possibly been involved with, given I was over at Lassen National Park the day before. Oh, and there's that other reason...I didn't even know your brother."

"My initial thought was off, as I suspected."

"About what? Graves?"

"No, you. Don't give me any crap about being a business consultant to Western corporations in Africa since I can count those on one hand, and they're not in Kenya. And by the way you took out those guys in the barn, it's more likely that you're with the State Department. I've crossed paths with those guys over the years who were pretending to be with an NGO or consulting, only to be involved in arming militants or whichever insurgent group our government needed on their side that month."

"And I've crossed paths with some world-weary journalists whose work has left them jaded to the core." He nodded back in the direction of McG's property. "Look, I get that you might be unhinged right now, especially after discovering Graves' role in your brother's death, but I'm not a part of the problem. I'll go with you to the sheriff's department, and we can explain what we uncovered at the creek along with Graves' admission, though I'm still unsure why Wayland needed your brother out of the way." He pursed his lips. "You obviously have more pieces of the puzzle than I do. Care to share?"

"Tell me what your interest is in all of this. Why are you even here, Kyle? I know you said something about taking a sightseeing trip, but why bury your nose in a case that doesn't even concern you?"

"When I saw the red clay on your brother's boots after Monroe stopped by the crime scene, I was curious, and frankly, I felt like Hanson was dragging his ass, so I began looking into things on my own in case he had plans to circle back to me as a suspect. Talking with Paige at her pottery gallery sent me off on a hunt for the answers since she knew the location of the clay sources." He rubbed the back of his neck. "But now, after what just happened at Graves' place, and the fact he was planning to add us to his compost pile out back, I'm just downright pissed. If there's one thing I can't stand, it's the corruption that comes with power-hungry corporations like Wayland that think they can stamp out anyone in their way. And whatever they're planning, I can almost guarantee it extends far beyond Absynth and McG's dope farms."

Eva studied his face for a moment. "I'm still not sure who you are, but I agree with a lot of what you just said. Let's get back to town and run all this by Monroe. Besides you, she's about the only person I trust right now."

"You're kidding? After all the shit you just gave me?"

"You saved my life back in that barn. Maybe you and Monroe can help me figure the rest of this out." She turned on her engine and accelerated, heading downhill and on an easterly route in the direction of town.

Payne followed behind, wondering what would come from poking the Wayland Corporation and a drug baron with his tentacles spread throughout the county. All he could think about was how he and Eva both had bullseyes on their backs that would only grow larger when they set foot in Absynth with the disturbing revelations of why Aaron Daly had met his end.

Except, Payne had a few targets of his own in mind now.

————

MONROE HAD JUST PULLED in behind the sheriff's department when she heard the roar of ATVs coming towards the parking lot. She stared in amazement at the two mud-streaked riders, sure she was dreaming. Only the bloody laceration on Payne's right shoulder told her the two hadn't been out sightseeing in the woods.

"What the hell happened?" she said as they stopped next to her vehicle, killing their engines.

"Graves…it was Matt Graves and his guys," said an exasperated Eva. "They grabbed us by a streambank near Wayland's facility."

Monroe swept her attention to Payne's face. "Please don't tell me you ensnared Eva in your theory about the clay deposits around town?"

"I was out there on my own when she showed up out of the blue."

Monroe frowned, looking at Eva for confirmation.

"It's true. I remembered seeing that red clay on Aaron's boots when you showed me his items downstairs, and when I was at my brother's place earlier, I realized from a previous text he sent me where he must have been on the day he died."

"How did you cross trails with Graves?" asked Monroe. "That part of the valley by Wayland's is outside of his turf, from what I know."

Payne got off the ATV. "He's on Wayland's payroll, providing muscle and security around their facility. Whatever they're up to at that place, they sure don't want anyone to know about it."

"Graves admitted to killing Aaron," said Eva as she dragged a sleeve across her moist eyes. "All for a bag of cash from Wayland."

Monroe scrunched her eyebrows together. "Wow, this just keeps getting crazier. I never would have put those two groups together." She rested a hand on Eva's shoulder. "I'm sorry."

Eva thrust her chin towards the western horizon. "He's at a homestead on the other side of Pittman Mountain. We were lucky to get away."

She glanced at Payne's shoulder with a bloody incision ringed with dirt. "How *did* you get away?"

Payne and Eva exchanged knowing glances. Payne leaned back against the ATV. "You know that sign on the road just before you enter Absynth...well, the population here just went down slightly."

Monroe folded her arms. "You killed Graves and his guys?"

"No, not *el jefe*, just a few of his dregs, including that knuckle-dragger Merle. He was holed up there. And Graves' barn full of product went up in flames. Whichever town is to the west of his place is going to have a lot of people missing work tomorrow from their coming buzz."

Monroe sighed, rubbing the back of her neck. "Damnit, Payne, this isn't a war zone."

He sent her a fierce gaze. "It is, actually, and the sooner you realize that, the better. Besides, those guys came after us. Like Eva said, we were damn lucky."

He thrust his arm towards the forest. "Whatever is going on in the sticks around here is about more than just growing dope. Graves and Wayland and Aaron Daly's murder are all connected."

Eva swung her leg around, sitting on the side of her ATV. "He's right. Graves flat-out told us he was getting paid by Wayland to provide security around their facility. The streambed with the red clay that butts up against their property is the last place Aaron was before he died. I'm sure of it. He stumbled onto something Wayland was doing and paid with his life." She stood, shuffling closer to Monroe. "You and Hanson need to get the feds involved."

Monroe glanced up at the thick cloud cover and the darkening sky. "I'll get ahold of the sheriff tonight and fill him in and then send word up the pipeline to the DEA office in Redding. We're just not equipped to storm into Graves' place. And with the roads about to be washed out tomorrow, any assault upon his place is probably going to have to wait until Monday."

"Graves will be gone by then, and whatever Wayland is up to will vanish," said Eva.

"Look, I understand you wanting to go after these guys, but locating your brother's tracks by that streambed isn't going to get a judge to sign off on a search warrant of the Wayland facility. Graves' kidnapping and how he assaulted you two is another story and is actionable."

Monroe removed her cellphone. "Is there anything you two need from me before I call Hanson? Where are your vehicles?"

"Back at the pullout along Verde Creek," said Eva.

"If they're still there," said Payne. "Probably hauled off by Graves' guys right after they grabbed us."

"I could use a ride back to my brother's house, where I'm staying."

"And you're at the field station, is that right?" Monroe said to Payne, who nodded. He noticed Eva give him a surprised look at his lodging.

"You sure you want to stay in the boonies without a vehicle right now?" Monroe asked him.

"Better than being stuck in that fleabag motel again, where I can't hear my enemies coming...and they will be coming for all of us." He made eye contact with both women. "Make no mistake, we all know now that Aaron was silenced, which means that the Wayland Corporation and Graves have a secret, and they'll kill to protect it."

"Neither of you is going to be safe at those locations, especially all alone. I've got a spare bedroom at my place that you can use, Eva. And Payne, you're welcome to crash on a cot in my enclosed porch. That should be quite a step up from your hammock and those musty beds in the field station dorms."

"That's very gracious of you, Becky, but I don't want to put you out, or put you at risk," said Eva.

"You're not. Plus I'll rest easier knowing you two are not sitting ducks."

Payne accepted the offer, knowing she was right. He just hoped she had some extra firepower on hand at her place because this had the potential to be a long night.

———

McG STOOD IN THE MEADOW, staring at the smoldering ruins of his barn, which had been a fixture on his uncle's property for decades. Now, a quarter of his crop was up in smoke. While he lamented the financial setback, he had a deep pit in his heart at the loss of Toko.

He heard his new second-in-command come up beside him. Ron Petrie handed him the tablet that showed the aerial footage of their drones. "Once they made it to the blacktop, they headed east towards town."

McG figured as much. He slapped the tablet back into

Petrie's chest. "This place is going to be swarming with DEA once things get relayed to the feds down south. With this coming storm, that probably won't be tonight or even tomorrow. No way they can get birds in the air or even handle the muddy roads out here, most of which will be washed out soon."

He glanced back at the porch of the two-story house, where his aunt and uncle were staring in sorrow at the remains of their beloved barn. "I need to get them out of here. I'm gonna grab our laptops and critical gear, then drive them down to my cousin's place in Weaverville. In the meantime, I want you to round up the other nearby crews and have them meet at our secondary property on the northeast side of the valley. I should be there around midnight."

"Roger. What's the plan after that?"

He had already mulled over his options and consulted his uncle. His ailing family were too frail to live on the run, and McG had no desire to disappear and assume a new identity in another state or country while leaving his aunt and uncle to suffer the consequences of his actions.

Plus, he figured with Wayland's reach, Theo Davenport's henchmen would track him down and put a bullet in his skull for compromising his operation. Right now, Graves knew he had a narrow window during the next forty-eight hours to eliminate the loose ends that threatened his family and his existence.

"I need information regarding the whereabouts of Eva Daly, that motherfucker Payne, and anyone else they talked to. But first I need to get ahold of my contact to find out if they've seen anything about the DEA rolling into town. If the feds haven't made a move after I get back from Weaverville, you, me and the rest of our crew are going on a little hunt."

CHAPTER 29

AFTER STEPPING INSIDE THE SHERIFF'S DEPARTMENT WHILE Monroe made some calls, Payne changed his dressing in the restroom. The cut hadn't gone as deep as he'd feared, and the median deltoid only had a laceration just beyond the surface.

He always dreaded knife fights. There were too many variables beyond one's control, and close-range combat with an edged weapon always meant that even the person surviving the fight could walk away maimed for life.

When he was done applying some Steri-Strips, he joined Eva in the employee break room, where the redheaded secretary was pulling two mugs with hot chocolate from the microwave.

"You always work this late?" he asked Dottie, who placed the steaming mugs on the table.

"Some days more than others. Just had a lot of paperwork to finish since next week is going to be all about storm damage and cleanup efforts."

Payne sipped on his beverage as the slender older woman slid a plate of toasted Pop-Tarts onto the table. "Let me ask you something...from what I heard the other day when you were talking to folks in the lobby, it sounds like you grew up here…you must know all the local stories, old and new."

Dottie sat down across from them. "That I do. I know everybody and all their dirty laundry too, sometimes more than I wish I did."

"What do you make of this recent tale about the Ghost?"

She pursed her lips, twirling the plate and staring at it like it was an oracle. "Not much. Started hearing the rumors last summer. It was connected with the wilderness areas west of town, three different canyons, in fact."

Eva broke off the corner of a Pop-Tart, sliding it into her mouth as she spoke. "I've been out of the loop here…what's the Ghost story about?"

"From what I gathered, it's an urban legend about something that preys upon hikers and hunters in the woods," said Payne.

Dottie shook her head. "None of those types went missing. No, sir. The four people whose bodies were found all had criminal records."

"Really, I hadn't heard that," said Payne.

"Probably seasonal dope harvesters," said Eva.

"What does Hanson think?" inquired Payne. "Could this be rival cartels knocking off their competition's workforce?"

The secretary shrugged her shoulders. "Yes. No. Who knows? There've been so many missing people in NorCal my entire life. Most of it's connected with the drug trade, but one thing that was odd is these fellas were all of Filipino descent."

"What was the cause of death for each one?" asked Eva.

Dottie canted her head. "All the same… rifle shots to the head. If I recall correctly from the reports I typed up, it was an uncommon caliber."

"Have there been any further cases like those?" inquired Payne.

"No, thankfully," said Dottie. "Becky, I mean Deputy

Monroe, has enough on her hands just trying to keep things running smoothly without all that."

"Isn't that Sheriff Hanson's job?" said Eva.

"Yeah, sure thing, sweetie," said the older woman as she stood, patting Eva on the shoulder and walking out.

Monroe reappeared, leaning a shoulder against the doorframe. "The DEA in Redding is going to send a crew up this way as soon as they can. They're currently running support operations for a big drug bust outside of Sacramento, so it's not likely they'll get here until after the storm."

"And Graves has disappeared," said Payne.

"Urban ops usually take precedence over small-town cases," the deputy bemoaned.

———

THE DRIVE to Monroe's house was less than fifteen minutes away. The place was tucked down a dead-end road with only three other properties on it. Hers was the second to last and nestled in the pines. The trees were so thick that Payne wondered if sunlight ever reached the ground.

Monroe pulled her Bronco into the gravel driveway, which extended for a hundred yards beyond the county road, parking in front of a two-bedroom home with cedar siding that she said had been built by her grandfather in the 1950s.

Along the left side was an aluminum carport with a fiberglass travel trailer inside, along with a workbench whose surface had a layer of fresh leaves that had blown inside.

Payne exited the Bronco, hearing a red squirrel chattering its disapproval from the trees above. The air smelled of burning wood and conifers, and he could see a wisp of smoke emanating from the stovepipe coming out of the stone chimney on the right side of the house.

Monroe led them up the steps of the enclosed porch where

Payne would be staying. He glanced at two old recliners before a long table, which had a conch-shell ashtray with a few cigar butts in it.

"Am I the only tenant?" he said, pointing to the ashtray.

"Sorry, I forgot to clear those out. My uncle comes over every Sunday, and we sit out here hemmin' and hawin' about how to save the world," said Monroe.

She unlocked the front door. The pleasant aroma of oak firewood wafted over them as they entered.

Monroe flicked on the living room lights. The ceiling was low, and the floor had been recently tiled with light tan linoleum. Payne paused in the entrance, seeing that the first photo on the wall was of Monroe's brother. Except in this image he was probably ten years younger, with some peach fuzz above his lip, and wearing a green graduation cap.

She waved her hand towards the hall on the left. "Bathroom and shower are at the end, so help yourselves. My bedroom is the last one and, Eva, you can take the room before that."

The dining room and kitchen were on the right along with a half-bath and laundry room near the side door. "Payne, I'll get out the cot and sleeping bag from the attic after I take care of the heat in here."

She moved to the left corner and pried open the woodstove door, stuffing in three leg-sized pieces of split oak from the woodpile against the wall, then adjusting the damper in the pipe.

"You guys hungry?" she asked, glancing at both of them as she brushed the bark off her hands.

"Pizza's on me," said Payne.

"Pff, trust me, you don't want to eat anything from the pizzeria in town," said Monroe.

"Is it still owned by that Polish family?" asked Eva.

Monroe said, "Regrettably. And they still add, like, four

inches of cheese to those cardboard slabs. Same style that they've been serving since our high-school days."

"Hungry tourists living on gas-station food probably don't complain, though," said Payne.

"But I have something better." Monroe headed to the kitchen, pulling out two packages of lasagna from the freezer. "Why don't you guys prep these. There should be some garlic bread in the freezer, too. I gotta make some more calls and then shower."

"Thanks for the hospitality, Becky," said Eva.

"I second that," said Payne, feeling like he was going to be the odd one out if the two old friends started recounting their youth and playing catchup. Then it dawned on him that it might work to his advantage, especially if he encouraged things along, since it would deflect from them probing too much into his life.

———

AN HOUR LATER, the smell of lasagna seemed to fill every inch of the living room. Payne and Eva sat on the two couches across from each other with their boots off, recounting the strange turn of events with Graves and their harrowing escape.

After a period of silence, Eva leaned in. "So why are you staying at the field station?"

"Another long story."

She waved a hand at their surroundings. "We have the time."

"One of the reasons I came here at all was to take an animal-tracking class with Tommy Larkin. He's someone I've wanted to learn from for a long time."

"The old cougar hunter? Why the interest?"

"My dad's a game warden in the Upper Peninsula of

Michigan, and I grew up tracking and hunting. I read Larkin's book on cougar ecology years ago and always swore that if I was out this way, I'd look him up. When things went to hell at that campground with Merle and his goons, my motorcycle took a hit. A couple of days ago, I ran into Larkin, and he told me the class was canceled but that I could stay out at the field station until next weekend when he was going to reschedule the event."

She opened up her arms. "That gorgeous valley always made me feel like I was being welcomed into the countryside."

"Spent a lot of time in that region?"

"My grandfather took Aaron and me there when we were little. The first time was at night. We drove up in his old truck that had chunks of rust falling off it. He stopped in the middle of the valley. It was pitch black. He had us lie on the grass while he pointed out the Big Dipper, Polaris, Cassiopeia, and how we could use them to find our way."

She rested her chin on her knee. "I've often thought that whenever I've felt lost in my life it's because there are too many clouds in my day...too many distractions, and when I clear all those away, I'll be able to see the stars again and find my way back to what's important."

He smiled. "You're a writer alright." But her words struck a chord in him. He'd had too many years of black clouds hanging over his own life in recent years with his precarious occupation. Until recently. And while he wasn't sure how long he would be a nomad, he had never felt as free. At least until arriving in Absynth.

"How did you end up in journalism and being an international correspondent?"

"When my forebearers settled in this region, my great-grandfather was a cattleman. Eventually, he turned over that part of the family business to his younger brother and became a rum-runner, hijacking other alcohol smugglers along the old route leading down from Oregon since he knew all the old wagon routes and horse trails. He had tunnels all over this town where he kept his stash. Once Prohibition ended, he opened a string of liquor and convenience stores from here down to Weaverville. With the wealth he accumulated, he was able to fund his rise to becoming the mayor, if you can believe that."

"Damn, that's some family history."

"Anyway, his son, my grandfather, avoided his father's notoriety and was the first person in our extended family to go to college in San Diego on a writing scholarship. Gramps bounced around newspapers for several years before using his inheritance to start his own newspaper in Redding. I was just a kid then, but I practically grew up in that building on Placer Street."

"Is that where your interest in writing started?"

"It sure didn't start with my own father, who was a gambler. Having a moral compass in my family seems to skip every other generation."

She tucked her knees into her chest. "When I was sixteen, I got an internship at Gramps' paper and never looked back. He was the one who helped me land a job at the *LA Times* after I graduated from journalism school."

Monroe emerged from her bedroom in sweats and a baggy shirt, running a towel over her damp hair. "Did she tell you about how she was a fricking combat journalist over in Syria and Africa and God knows where else?"

Eva grinned. She glided her fingers over her wooden pendant. "Payne's been in Africa. He knew all about this carved image. Said it was from his time in Kenya, consulting." She clawed out air quotes at the mention of the latter word.

"Risk-management consultant…that's what he told me when we first met. I mean, when I arrested his ass."

"It was your little gopher, Kessel, actually, who did the arresting. You just stood there, counting the minutes until you could get back here for a nap."

"Haha. Kessel's not my gopher; he's just green."

"I remember him being mostly red in the face," said Payne with a frown.

Eva stretched out her legs. "Becky, have you noticed that Payne likes to subtly shift the conversation away from himself to avoid answering questions? And he's good at it, too."

"Oh, yeah, I observed that from the get-go."

Eva said, "He did that earlier when I mentioned that the only Americans I knew in Kenya were with the State Department."

Payne lay back on the couch, resting his hand across his chest. "I'm starting to feel like I'm back in that mildewy inter- rogation room at the sheriff's department."

Eva nudged him with her foot. "So, by my estimate, from what I've gathered from Becky and what I witnessed myself, you have put quite a dent in the local lowlife population since arriving here. It seems like it was largely self-defense, but what's the real story on your background, Payne?"

Monroe sat on the recliner, staring at him. "Yeah, Kyle, care to elaborate?"

He hopped to his feet, grabbing a towel off the back of the couch. "It's an epic tale for another time, but thanks for your interest." He headed into the bathroom, closing the door and hoping that the entryway on his own past would remain sealed until he left town.

––––––––

"I LOST DALY," said Schulz.

"Explain," replied Wagner on his encrypted iPhone while scrolling through Hanson's laptop in the sheriff's living room.

"After she left her brother's house, Eva drove to a forested area not far from Wayland's research site. There was some other guy there too. They must have been meeting since they arrived about the same time. That's where it gets interesting…a bunch of armed men surrounded them and drove off with Daly and her buddy."

"Wayland's guards?"

"There were a few guards, but the rest looked like militia or biker types. And they drove north away from the Wayland facility. We followed for a few miles, but then they veered down a narrow dirt road and disappeared."

"*Shiza!*" Wagner gripped the phone tighter. "Davenport mentioned something about partnering with a local drug dealer. My next stop was going to be the Wayland site to talk with their security chief, so I'll find out where Eva was taken."

"You and Elke still at the sheriff's place?"

"Yeah, the old dog took a while to break, but we're going through his place for any files related to the Daly case."

Wagner glanced at his watch. "Head back to town and get inside the county records building on Third Street. I want you to dig up any old maps that show where the Daly family had their properties around town. From what I could find online, many of them have been sold over the years, but the older holdings might show up in the county archives."

"When do you want me to hack into the telecoms and repeater towers to shut things down?" asked Regal in the background.

Wagner mulled over the ever-shifting timeline in his head. "Let's plan for tomorrow morning, but I'll let you know in a few hours once I get a feel for where Aaron Daly's trail of breadcrumbs leads us."

CHAPTER 30

THE DRIVE OUT TO THE FIELD STATION WITH MONROE WAS punctuated by both women sharing their stories about the area and natural wonders, making Payne feel like he was with two professional tour guides.

Pulling up to the driveway that wound up to the dining hall, Payne saw Larkin and a forty-something man raking woodchips onto the walkways.

"That must be Gary, the caretaker," said Monroe.

"You've never met him?" asked Payne.

"He just started a few months ago. Only comes into town once or twice a month," the deputy replied.

Payne was expecting a spry figure who handled the physical maintenance of the property, but Gary's overweight pear-shaped appearance and pale skin made Payne wonder how much time the man actually spent outside.

"Hard to get someone to stay out here full time," said Monroe. "Tommy told me Gary used to own a couple of townhomes in Weed and had plenty of experience with plumbing and construction, so he got the job."

Strange going from the city to living way out here. Wonder if the guy is running from something...or someone.

They exited the Bronco and headed up to the dining hall, exchanging introductions.

Monroe checked her phone again, then grabbed the two-way radio from her belt, calling Kessel. He was on the other end of the county, closing off the last of the dirt roads, and was at least an hour drive away from Absynth, according to what Payne overheard.

When she'd finished, Monroe slid her radio back on her belt. "I can't get ahold of Hanson, so I'm going to spin out to his house and see if he's alright. He might just be knocked out from his pain meds, but it worries me."

"You want me to come along?" said Larkin.

"No, I know you and Gary have things to take care of before these walkways turn to mush in the rain. I should be back in a couple of hours."

Monroe headed down the driveway to her vehicle, then sped off down the road in such a way that everyone's attention was focused on her.

"You need help with anything?" Payne asked Larkin.

"Nah, just gotta throw some tarps over the hay bales out back and finish securing the windows on the dorms, but thanks all the same. I'd just go enjoy yourselves on the property before the biblical flood arrives."

The two men ambled towards Larkin's Chevy pickup, leaving Eva and Payne standing under the immense pine tree near the dining hall.

"Take a walk with me," she said. Eva turned and headed up the trail, not waiting to hear his response.

She walked past the row of dorms and continued straight into the knee-high grass, leading him up a gentle slope into the forest.

"You're not going to get me lost, are you? 'Cause I left my survival kit in my cabin."

"Haha, you seem like you'd be at home almost anywhere."

He glanced beyond her at the thick forest. "Where are we going, exactly?"

She pushed on, cresting the hill and pausing at the top. Eva pointed to a bowl-shaped meadow below. "Remember when I mentioned that my grandfather brought Aaron and me out here to stargaze when we were kids? Well, this land and the buildings once belonged to my family. The structures by the vehicles were the ranch headquarters for his father's cattle operation back in the day. When ranching faded in these parts, my grandfather donated 270 of the 290 acres to the natural history foundation in Redding, which then worked with a number of universities throughout California to turn it into a center for ecological field studies."

Payne gazed at the tranquil setting below, spying a log cabin tucked into the trees like it had sprung from the earth. "And these are the remaining twenty acres?"

She nodded, but before he could probe further, she trotted down the grassy slope, skipping at times like she was a child again as her slender fingers brushed along the tops of wilted flower stalks.

Payne followed behind her until they arrived at the back porch of the modest abode. The place had a cedar-plank roof with a stone chimney on one side. The thick log walls still had the old ax marks, and the faded chinking looked like it was an adobe mix of mud and straw. The only modern intrusion was a metal generator box on the ground to the right along with some gas cans.

He heard a faint chirping sound emanating from under the eaves and pointed up to a gap in the façade. "We've interrupted the bats' sleep."

She gave him a surprised glance. "Very good. Not many people would know what that sound means. Guess you're not the urban cowboy I first took you for."

"I grew up in a small town in northern Michigan, surrounded by swamps and forest. It'd make Absynth feel like Sacramento."

Eva lifted the lid on a wooden birdhouse nailed to the right of the door. She removed a tarnished key and used it to unlock the door before heading inside.

The odor of wood smoke and some kind of chemical wafted over them. Payne heard something scurry away in the left corner and saw a gray mouse dart behind some cardboard boxes.

"This used to be the ranch foreman's place, but Aaron took it over a few years ago, using it for a mini-lab to store his fieldwork and books." Eva moved to each of the six windows, parting the tattered curtains so the weak daylight could penetrate the interior. She immediately zeroed her attention on the stacks of notebooks and a laptop beside the desk.

"Who else knows about this place?"

"Tommy Larkin, I imagine the caretaker, and now you. Being a science geek, Aaron always thought of this cabin as his secret laboratory."

She waved to a small dining table near some cupboards and a kitchen counter. "If he was really caught up in his work, then he even spent the night. I remember one time, he…" Her voice trailed off.

Eva leaned on the desk, her lips trembling as she gazed over his possessions. "God, he loved this place and the work he did."

Payne rested a hand on her shoulder. "Maybe there are some answers here that will help figure out what he discovered out by the Wayland site."

She nodded, sniffling and wiping her hand across her

moist cheeks. She grabbed the top notebook on the pile and handed it to Payne. "Why don't you look through that while I see what's on his computer. It's been plugged into a portable battery, so it should still have some juice."

Payne took the spiral-bound notebook to the table and sat down. He scanned the last few entries, which were marked in pencil with the date and time. It took him a while to translate Daly's horrendous handwriting, but it was clear that his focus had been entirely on his fieldwork near the Wayland facility.

Found another specimen with the white fungus on its posterior, identical to the one I sent off to Gabe. Should know more soon but looks pretty conclusive to me that this is not an aberration. But what the hell is Cryptolestes pusillus doing in this part of the world?

The day before Aaron was killed, there was another entry that piqued Payne's interest.

Upon closer inspection of the crop sample I obtained with the beetles, it also doesn't appear to be endemic to North America. I need to go back out to the Wayland site tomorrow and collect some additional plant stalks to send to Gabe. His botanists should be able to confirm my findings.

And the last morning before he died, his final entry was terse.

After a restless night worrying about the implications of my findings, I am just going to gather more specimens at the site and drive down to Gabe's lab to fast-track this. I believe Wayland designed a genetically engineered strain of Claviceps purpurea fungus that can be transmitted via the common European grain beetle. If I'm right, then the alarm

*has to be sounded on what Wayland's doing. I just hope I'm
in time, or this could have catastrophic implications.*

"You should see this," said Eva in a pensive voice.

Payne set down the journal, walking over to her. There
was shaky Go-Pro camera footage of someone narrating as
they moved briskly along a narrow footpath in the woods.

"Aaron's talking. This is time-stamped a week before he
died." She turned up the volume. "Pretty sure this is where it
all began for him."

Aaron moved a white mesh net through the tall grasses
just outside a fence line posted with a no-trespassing sign
below the Wayland logo.

He slid back the six-foot handle of the bug-collecting net
and reached inside, removing a handful of grasshoppers,
ladybugs and one elongated brown beetle. With the exception
of the latter, he gently returned the others to the grass.

Aaron popped open a narrow glass vial and inserted the
beetle before closing the lid. *"This little guy looks out of place.
Never even seen one except in European entomology field guides. It
appears it has some strain of fungus on its exoskeleton. Normally, a
fungal infection of this magnitude would have killed its host by
now, but it seems unaffected. If this is the fungus I believe it is, then
it would decimate the wheat crops in Europe in a matter of
months."*

He panned his camera out to the sunlit fields of glistening
crops on the other side of the Wayland fence line. There was
movement of people a few hundred yards beyond the wheat
stalks by the Wayland agro-facility. The camera shook, the
view suddenly going from the field to the ground, as Aaron
must have ducked down. *"Were they yelling at me? This is
national forest land on this side of the fence, you dipshits."*

The rest of the footage was of Aaron trotting back through
the woods to his vehicle, after which the camera shut down.

Eva slumped back in her seat, a deflated look on her face. "What did you get yourself into, big brother?"

"Your brother's journal entries indicate similar findings. He also mentioned that the wheat in Europe is a different strain than the type found here in North America. Wayland has invented some type of fungal bioweapon it plans to unleash upon Europe."

"And with them controlling the lion's share of wheat production in this country, they will monopolize global distribution. Hell, they may even have a cure for the disease they could say they came up with to sell to European nations. Either way, they stand to make billions off of this."

Payne sat on the edge of the desk. "Tell me more about the Wayland place and how they came to be this far out from their headquarters in LA."

"They started up here about eight years ago, as I recall. The property was actually one of my family's holdings back in the day. That old brick building used to house my great-grandfather's liquor during the Prohibition. All I know is the locals were excited when Wayland first talked about setting up shop here because it would mean more jobs. Except for a couple of townies, Wayland brought in a few dozen of their own people from LA instead. Some of them rent in town, and others live in trailers on the property."

"And what were you told they were doing, exactly?"

"They've got a bunch of satellite agro-sites around the Western US, and according to what Aaron told me years ago, each facility is in a different biome so they can see how wheat production is affected by soil types and climate. He actually applied for a job with them three years ago but never heard back."

She waved a hand at his research materials. "Why the hell wouldn't you want a local who is a top-notch scientist working for you? He probably knows ten times more than any of their staff." Eva balled a fist. "Knew...he knew. Fuck!"

"Because he stumbled onto something with global implications. He even alludes to it in his journal entries. And if his findings panned out, he was going to blow the whistle on Wayland. It sounds like this goes far beyond what they are doing on their little plot of land out here. Why else would they suddenly employ Graves and his goons to provide security? But what's Wayland's end game?"

"Theo Davenport is the CEO. He lives in LA, and his company controls the lion's share of wheat distribution in this country."

Payne retrieved Aaron's notebook from the table, showing Eva his entries. "Do you know what came of the specimens Aaron sent to this guy Gabe?"

"Not sure. I was supposed to meet with Gabe a few days ago, but he hasn't been returning my calls, and his colleagues didn't know where he's at. I'm worried that something's happened to him as well, now."

"The outcome of that specimen sounds like it could really help us dial in this investigation."

Eva let her eyes linger over the journal, then glanced up at Payne. "'Us'...why are you so eager to join this fight? Is this about that latter word, 'fight'; is that where you thrive, Kyle? Like an adrenaline junkie. And why would you even lift a finger to help out with the way you were treated in this town?"

He set down the journal, folding his arms. Payne was drawn in by her sorrowful eyes, determining how to word his desire to take down Graves and also help her find justice for what happened to Aaron. "There used to be this small family operation of loggers near where I grew up. The Burns family. They were a bunch of cutthroats and bullies who used to go into other loggers' sites and drive metal spikes into the trees so their competitors would get maimed when their chainsaws hit one of those spikes. Lots of guys ended up with permanent injuries and jagged scars on their faces when the spinning blade recoiled back at them.

"Most people knew it was the Burns fellas. I went to high school with the two youngest boys, and they were always getting suspended for harassing girls on the walk home. At some point, it seems that somebody poured sugar into all the gas tanks of their chainsaws and their pickup trucks and their tractors just before Burns had a big timber-harvesting contract to fulfill. The old man found himself out of business, and he and his yellow rat-bastard sons had to relocate to Minnesota."

She scrutinized his face. "They ever find who vandalized the stuff?"

"The sheriff never launched an investigation, so no."

"Sounds like all those Burns boys had it coming."

He thrust his chin at the video. "So should some others, don't you think?"

"Look, I'm all about getting justice for what happened to my brother, and certainly Graves needs to be behind bars for what he did, but what you're talking about is vigilante justice, and that's not what I had in mind. Not to mention that Hanson and Monroe aren't going to let you just steamroll over them."

Payne rapped his knuckles on the notebook. "Your brother states in there that he suspects Wayland is planning something that could have a ripple effect upon the world. Something like that is not undertaken with chump change. It requires a network and is probably a billion-dollar operation. You really think Hanson slapping some cuffs on the Wayland guys is going to put a halt to their plans or provide retribution for what happened to your brother?"

"You're forgetting who I work for. If I can expose Wayland

publicly in the media, that can hamstring them and their operations."

He shook his head, pacing beside the desk. "Here's a more likely scenario: Wayland completes their objective at their facility down the road, then burns the place to the ground along with the nonessential staff. Then they send a kill squad to take out Graves and anyone else familiar with his role at the Wayland property. Afterwards, they mop up in town, eliminating any other loose ends like Monroe or Hanson...or you. The next day, all the hitmen disappear, and Wayland blackmails, threatens or bribes guys like your boss at the *LA Times* so they don't ever run a story. Or if they do, it will be about a rogue group of scientists in Absynth who were planning their own little op with some European counterparts. And your brother and his boss Gabe are implicated as accomplices."

He leaned both hands on the desk, clenching the sides and staring straight into her eyes. "Look, I know how these kinds of people work because I was the guy sent in by our government to eliminate them before they could unleash their horrors on the world."

She leaned back in her seat, her mouth hanging open. "So I was right all along. You were a fucking spook." Eva slammed the laptop closed, then swiveled towards him. "Who were you with...the CIA, Defense Intelligence, JSOC?"

"Does it matter?" He waved a hand towards the forest outside the windows. "I'm done with that kind of work and all that goes with it. At least, I thought I was done with most of it until I showed up here. Now, I have no plans to leave until Wayland's and Graves' operations are dismantled."

"Even if that means laying waste to more of Graves' people or the guys on the other side of the Wayland fence line?"

"I'll burn that bridge to the ground when I get to it."

CHAPTER 31

THE DRIVE BACK TO ABSYNTH WAS ONLY TWENTY MILES, BUT IT seemed like it took an hour. Monroe's head felt like it had a splinter in the side from the lack of sleep and the growing tension from the past few days.

She grabbed the police radio mic off the console but didn't have any luck reaching dispatch, Kessel, or Hanson.

Wonder if the repeater tower on the mountain is down from the winds. She dismissed the idea, knowing there were several towers scattered around Absynth, and they had withstood far greater winds than what was currently rolling in. Besides, her iPhone's reception had suddenly dropped off, which made her think this was a larger region-wide problem that possibly emanated out of the statewide comms relay center in Redding.

But why would Verizon also be affected?

She pushed her vehicle fifteen miles past the speed limit, eager to get to Hanson's place and seek his advice. While he was often ornery and certainly cynical, his experience as a lawman was what she needed most right now.

Monroe had dealt with her share of miscreants, dope peddlers and thieves during her eight-year stint with the sheriff's department, but whatever blight had infested Absynth in the past week was about more than the bizarre murder of Aaron Daly. And with Graves' outright admission of his involvement and his escalation to kidnapping, he was going to have to be apprehended. If he were a lone fugitive, that would present its own challenges, but with his small army of guys, Monroe didn't want a full-scale regional war on her hands.

And why did he kill Aaron in the first place? What did Aaron discover?

She thought about Eva's arrival and their subsequent time together.

What's she not telling me? Eva was always so chatty, but now seems so guarded. Is that all connected with Aaron's death? Is there something else going on with her?

Four miles from town, Monroe took a right turn down a hard-packed dirt road that was already glistening from the intermittent showers that had started coming down in the past half hour. She drove south for two miles and made a left at the fork in the road that led to Hanson's place.

Turning into his gravel driveway, she headed down the winding road for a quarter mile, pulling up behind his truck.

She could see his horses gathered by the fence line, their heads bobbing frantically as they whinnied.

Weather got them spooked?

Monroe exited her Bronco, walking towards the front porch. A crimson stain on the sandstone pavers caused her to freeze. Her eyes followed the blood trail towards the tractor, where Jerry Hanson was slumped forward, his face and arms looking like they had been filleted.

Her sides constricted, and she felt like vomiting. Monroe trotted to her boss, shouting his name but knowing he would never again respond to her. The dozens of incisions on his arms, legs and neck made it seem like he had crawled through a field of razor wire.

She bent down, checking his pulse, but his skin felt leathery, and she wondered how long he'd been like this. *My God, who could do such a thing?*

With his death certain, she stood, removing her Sig Sauer service pistol and pressing her back to the tractor. The rain was coming down harder now, washing away the blood on the patio stones. She surveyed the front porch and upstairs windows, then swept her gaze out to the tack barn near the pasture.

Monroe headed up the front steps and into the house. The door was ajar, and by the amount of leaves that had blown inside and the dried mud, she suspected the killer was long gone.

She pulled the radio off her belt, trying to call Kessel, but only static ensued. She headed to Hanson's den on the right, remembering he had a landline. Except her call wouldn't go through since everyone she tried also had cellular service. Even dispatch at the sheriff's department was impossible to reach.

Shit, I'd be better off using a signal mirror. She smirked at the futility, since even that joke of a plan would be thwarted by the thick cloud cover.

Monroe walked through the rest of the house, seeing nothing of value had been stolen. Even his wallet and service pistol were sitting on the kitchen counter.

What the hell happened here? By his wounds, it's clear he was tortured. But why? Did Graves do this? She rubbed her temple, her headache intensifying. *It's just not his MO, but then neither is killing Aaron Daly or what he supposedly had in mind for Eva and Payne.*

Monroe headed out the back door, scanning the meadows,

then walking down to the barn. The double doors were closed, and she slowly opened one and swept inside with her pistol, clearing the stalls and the tack room at the end.

She heard the rustling of the horses outside and opened the side door, letting them in. The deputy was known to them, and each of them greeted her with a gentle sniff and brush against her side as they glanced around for their owner.

"I'm sorry, my sweet friends." Monroe wondered if they had seen what had unfolded and hoped for their sake that they had been far off in the meadow.

She holstered her pistol and removed her folding knife, slicing through the twine holding a large bale of green hay together. Monroe pulled out several clumps and tossed them onto the ground, then dispersed the rest around the stalls. Before she left, she checked that they had water and locked all the doors from the outside, knowing they would need shelter from the coming deluge.

On her way back to her vehicle, she paused beside Hanson. The thought of a prayer had crossed her mind, but she couldn't even recall the old words.

"Sorry, boss. It shouldn't have been this way, but you can be damn sure I'll find who did this."

———

THE DRIVE back to the main road was fraught with a dozen questions racing through Monroe's head as she raced towards Absynth.

A few minutes later, she pulled in at the rear of the sheriff's department.

"I was hoping you would show up soon, Deputy Monroe," said a man to her left near the dumpster. He was wearing a trench coat and had both hands in the pockets. He had a striking face with neatly combed black hair and hazel eyes.

For a second, she wondered if he was with the feds out of Redding, and if Eva had went around her authority and called for help with the Graves' situation.

"Is there somewhere we can talk?" he asked, stepping closer, the hint of a German accent evident. "I parked around the other side in case you're wondering. I'm working on a case regarding Aaron Daly and was told you're the person to speak with."

She rested her hand on her pistol, stepping towards the back door. "And who are you, exactly?"

"Someone interested in Aaron Daly, and if you want to live beyond today, then you'll stand still and put your hands by your sides." He motioned to her sternum.

Monroe glanced down at the red dot on her shirt, then out to the tree line at the edge of the parking lot.

"It'd be so tragic to die right on the doorstep of your own building. But then, the coroner wouldn't have a long walk to the crime scene."

"You're seriously threatening an officer. What the hell's going on?"

"I would burn through all of your colleagues inside if I thought I could get the answers I need. Except that would take too long. Your stoic sheriff felt the need to resist, which really made it a long night for all of us."

Monroe started to lunge forward, but something zinged past her ear, splintering the wood doorframe behind her.

He waved at the dangling security camera above the rear door. "I don't want to have to slaughter all your friends inside, who are oblivious to your dilemma, but I will unless you come with me right now."

"To where? What's this about?"

"Aaron Daly's research. He had something of great value to my employer, and now Eva is most likely in possession of it." He moved closer, resting his hand on her Sig Sauer and removing it along with her OC spray and Taser. "I need you to take me to her. Surely, you must know her location since Eva came to see you shortly after arriving in this quaint little town."

He interlaced his arm around her right elbow as he nudged her through the parking lot and around the other side, keeping the barrel of her service pistol pressed against her ribs.

"Hanson really was a tough old goat. He didn't give up much except to say that we'd have to reckon with you." He chuckled. "My Lord, that really struck terror into my heart. I almost left town."

"Fuck off."

He shoved her up against the side of a black Suburban, pressing the barrel of her pistol harder into her ribs until she winced.

A slender woman in a black leather jacket emerged from the woods with a backpack. By its elongated shape, Monroe figured she had a takedown sniper rifle inside.

The man frisked Monroe, removing her iPhone and waving it before her face. "We hacked into the local repeaters, cell towers and internet servers and rendered them useless. You and your pathetic sheriff's department and the rest of this cow hole are sealed off from the world. And with this storm about to shut down this entire part of the state, Absynth belongs to us now."

———

Deputy Kessel exited his work vehicle and donned his brimmed hat, trotting towards the café. He could have parked across the street at the sheriff's department and walked over, but he was already cold and wet from the past few hours of doing road closures and notifying people at nearby campgrounds about the upcoming weather conditions.

He paused in the lobby, shaking the droplets off his hat and sleeves, then headed towards Earl at the counter. Surprisingly, the place was fairly empty, and he figured most of the locals were preparing to ride out the storm at home.

He heard the clack of nails on the tiled floor and saw Bosco come around the curved side of the counter.

"How you doin', fella?" he asked, leaning over and stroking the dog's neck.

Paige got up from her table in the corner and sauntered over. "You go for a dunk in the river?" she asked.

"Haha, some of us actually work for a living instead of playing with dirt."

Earl moved to the counter. "It's clay, actually, or didn't you get the lecture from Paige yet? It's ninety-two percent clay and eight percent temper material of fine sand."

Kessel shrugged his shoulders. "Sorry, I missed that fascinating infomercial."

"What'll it be? You're holding up the line," quipped Earl.

The deputy pulled the radio off his belt, adjusting the volume. "How about some new batteries? Damn thing hasn't been working very well."

Earl reached over and grabbed it, adjusting the squelch before handing it back. "You guys seriously need to get some updated gear. That looks like the first model from 1940, for crying out loud."

"I don't think it's limited to just your radio," said Paige, who was thumbing the screen of her iPhone. "I haven't had internet for half an hour now."

Earl swiveled the tablet mounted on the counter. "Damn, my service is out too." He glanced through the front windows. "Maybe the lines got blown down from the high winds."

Paige smirked at him. "Nobody uses phone lines anymore. Wireless service operates off the cell towers in the region, old-timer."

The café owner chuckled, then shot a glance at Kessel. "You oughta arrest this juvenile for elder abuse."

The deputy ignored the banter and pulled out his personal iPhone, tapping on the screen. "Either of you seen or heard from the sheriff, or Monroe, for that matter?"

They both responded in the negative.

Kessel swiveled around, gazing across the street towards the sheriff's department. From this location, he could only make out a sliver of the right side of the building. He glimpsed Monroe getting into the back of a black Suburban, followed by a woman with a backpack and a tall man in a trench coat.

"Shit, are the feds up here already? I thought they weren't gonna be able to make it until Monday?"

"This about Aaron Daly's murder?" said Earl.

"What?" asked Paige. "Aaron's dead?"

"Sorry, I thought you knew," said the older man. "Heard about it yesterday."

"Heard from who?" asked Kessel.

"Like, three of my regulars…the usual ones who always jabber on about someone else's misfortunes so they can forget how miserable they are."

Kessel watched the Suburban turn out of the parking lot across the street and drive west. *Where the hell are they going?*

Earl had poured a cup of coffee with creamer into a Styrofoam cup and slid it across the counter towards Kessel along with a blueberry Danish in a paper bag. "On me, son."

"Thanks," said Kessel, putting a lid on the coffee and grabbing the sugary breakfast.

He headed to the door, stepping out into the rain and watching the Suburban disappear in the distance. *Such bullshit, keeping me out of my first investigation with the feds.*

CHAPTER 32

THE WALK BACK TO THE FIELD STATION WAS MARKED BY drenched boots and pants as Payne and Eva trudged up the rain-dappled slope from Aaron's cabin and down the other side towards the main camp.

Arriving at his cabin, he unlocked the door and went inside.

Eva deposited her brother's pack, containing his notebooks and laptop, on the small table in the corner, removing the flash drive of pertinent files she'd copied and sliding it into her pants pocket. "You hear that?" she asked, turning towards the open door.

Payne moved towards the entrance, leaning out and swiveling his head until he located the sound of the shouting. He walked towards the next cabin, which protruded ahead slightly from his own, and peered around the corner.

Monroe was standing between Larkin and Gary, their faces frozen in terror. A tall man in a trench coat was holding a suppressed pistol while barking questions at them. A second later, the man shot Gary in the head, splintering his skull onto the dining hall steps.

"Oh my God, what's happening?" muttered Eva, who was beside him.

He pulled her arm, moving back against the wall of the dorm. "That's a different caliber of bad guy than what we saw at Graves' place." He glanced back at the open door of his cabin. "They must be after your brother's research. The kill squad I mentioned."

"What now?"

He removed the Spyderco folding blade clipped in his pants pocket, wishing he were clutching his .38 snubbie. "Stay put while I move around the back side and see about—"

"Set your weapon down, and I won't blow your girl-friend's brains all over the ground," said a woman's voice from the woods by the rear of the dorm.

———

PAYNE STOOD in formation with the others in front of the dining hall, nestled between Monroe and Eva. Behind them was the limp figure of the plump caretaker, whose rivulets of blood were trickling in the rain along the walkway. From what Payne had gleaned from a conversation when the woman called her partner over, he went by Wagner.

"Find anything?" asked Wagner as he glanced at his female accomplice on the porch, who was sifting through Daly's notebooks.

Payne noted that they both had slight German accents, which further added to the mystery of the parties interested in Aaron Daly's work. He also noticed a black dove tattoo on the man's left inner wrist that further piqued his curiosity.

"He writes in one of the notebooks that he was onto the bug being developed, but that's all. Mentions that guy Gabe that you visited with."

Eva's face turned ashen at the mention of the latter name. "Please tell me you didn't…"

"Kill your pal Gabe and your BFF Bethany…of course not, we just chatted, and then they both promised not to call the police on me." The man sent a vicious backhand across Eva's face, dropping her to the ground.

Payne went to rush at him, but the man swung his HK pistol towards his forehead. "As for your role in all of this, it doesn't make sense from what you've told me, but I don't want to obliterate any more pieces from the chessboard just yet."

Wagner stepped back and removed a satellite phone from his trench coat, pressing a pre-saved number. "I think we've found Daly's files. Get over to my location. This appears to be ground zero for what we need, and it may take a while to tear this place apart; bring the security crew from Wayland so we can speed things up, and call me when you're inbound."

Payne figured that, since the guy had already eliminated a number of people, he planned to execute all of them after obtaining what he was looking for. The clock was ticking. But Payne had few options at his disposal. Except a new glimmer of hope had just materialized, and he had to carefully orchestrate the events of the next few minutes if he'd have a chance at a payoff.

"He's an animal," said Monroe, who helped up Eva. "I can't even describe what he did to Hanson."

"Not me per se," replied Wagner. "My compatriot, actually. Her blade work is far more exquisite than mine despite my attempts to emulate her." He waved his pistol towards the woman, telling her to examine the contents of the laptop they'd found in the daypack in Eva's possession.

"You're leaving quite a trail of dead bodies around the state," said Payne. "Since that doesn't seem to worry you, and with those German accents, I'd say you think you can operate with impunity. But what does worry you, and the employer yanking your chain, is the outside world discovering what Wayland has been formulating in their lab down the road."

"So you do know something."

Payne nodded at the man's wrist. "I know you were once with Schwarze Taube. What the hell would a former German black-ops guy be doing on our shores? Since Daly discovered a European beetle with a genetically engineered fungal infection, I'd say his theory was right about Wayland unleashing a nasty little bioweapon overseas."

Both the woman and Wagner paused to glance at each other. Wagner grinned, shooting a straight jab directly into Payne's solar plexus.

Payne felt his insides roil and dropped to one knee, marveling at the exquisite speed of the punch while trying to fight back the overpowering nausea.

"A better question is: who the hell are you with? If you know something about German covert ops, then you're either a former intelligence analyst or a contractor. Except it doesn't make sense you'd be out here with these cowpie lovers."

Payne staggered back to his feet, sucking in several deep breaths. He'd been stalling as long as he could, risking exposing his background to the others.

Just a few more seconds.

"Holy shit...found it," said the woman as she turned the laptop around, showing Aaron's video.

And then it unfolded, Payne watching in slow motion and waiting for the microsecond of opportunity.

"Freeze and put your weapons down," shouted Deputy Kessel, who stood up on the other side of the Suburban with his pistol pointed at Wagner.

"You got this?" whispered Wagner over his shoulder to his accomplice as he slowly turned towards the deputy.

"Yeah," replied the woman as she began walking along

the porch, her hand moving towards the back of her leather jacket.

Payne rushed at Wagner, who was angled slightly towards the Suburban. He drove his arms around the man's waist in a wrestler's clinch, dumping him sideways onto the ground. Payne scythed an elbow into the man's cheek, then slammed a hammer fist down onto the guy's weapon hand, dislodging the HK pistol. He immediately followed up with a vicious right hook to the German's face.

Payne heard gunshots around him but focused on the pistol, grabbing it and rolling onto his side, then squeezing off two rounds that struck the woman in the neck and lower jaw. She collapsed against the dining hall wall and slid to the ground.

Wagner leapt onto Payne, gripping his throat with one hand while using his other to begin wrestling down the gun.

A black blur sailed near Payne's face as Monroe sent a swift kick into the guy's head, dropping him onto the walkway.

Payne hopped up, staring at Eva's pale face as she pointed. "God, Kessel's been shot."

CHAPTER 33

IT WAS A GAPING SHOULDER WOUND, THE HOLLOW POINT shredding part of Kessel's right deltoid. He lay slumped against an upright post on the porch of the dining hall as Larkin applied a compress of kitchen towels. When Larkin finished, he removed a triangle bandage from the first-aid kit he'd obtained from inside the building and wrapped a sling around the deputy's arm.

"You were damn lucky that fella Payne shot that bitch, or your brains would be fertilizin' the forest," said Larkin.

"And we're all damn lucky Deputy Kessel showed up when he did," said Payne.

Kessel glanced up at Monroe. "Something didn't sit right with the way I saw you being escorted off earlier by these two. When you didn't respond on your radio, I figured I'd better trail behind."

"Well, your instincts paid off," said Monroe. "This would have had a totally different outcome if you hadn't showed up."

"We need to get him to the hospital and then get this laptop to the authorities up in Redding," said Eva.

Payne gazed down at the main road before turning his attention to Wagner, who had his hands cuffed to the porch railing. "How many guys are inbound?"

The man muttered something in German and spat on the ground.

Payne slid forward, kicking the man in the stomach. "How many?"

Wagner coughed, gasping for air before responding, "More than your little band of misfits can handle."

Payne sent the tip of his boot into the man's ribs. "Two more precise strikes like that and the ribs crack, and the lower rim of your right lung is punctured. Hell of a way to go, aspirating on your own blood."

Wagner's grimace turned to a faint grin. "You must have attended the same interrogation school as me."

Payne kicked him again with slightly more force. "I can work the left side too, if you'd like."

Wagner winced, letting out a bronchial cough. "Ten, maybe fifteen heavily armed guys."

"Payne, stop," said Monroe, shuffling closer. "He's my prisoner now, and I'm taking him back to the department."

He fixed his gaze on the deputy. "Is there another way out of here? A Forest Service road, maybe."

She shook her head. "Just the main road we came in on."

"That'll be a kill box if we attempt to get back to town that way. They'll pick us apart either there or on the main road, and they may have already dropped off a few shooters along the route as we speak."

"There's the Beachum Trail that heads north for five miles," said Larkin, thrusting a spear hand out to a trail-marker beyond the parking area. "It'd take us to Forest Road 334 and a coupla ranches out that way."

Payne did the rough calculations of foot travel in his head, knowing the average hiker could cover a minimum of two miles in under an hour. Add in Kessel, who was the weakest link, and they were looking at three hours of trekking. He glanced up at the faint glow of sunlight along the horizon and knew it would be a hard slog along wet trails, part of which would be in the dark.

"I still think we're better off taking our chances driving out right now," said Monroe. "We're not going to be much better off if we're all on that trail with a hell-bent team of shooters on our ass."

A grating sound near the entrance gate diverted their attention, and all of their heads swiveled in unison at the approaching convoy of three SUVs with dark-tinted windows.

"You were saying," Payne muttered as the vehicles came to a halt a mile out near the main gate.

He hopped off the porch and ran to the Suburban, rummaging through the interior. Payne unzipped a padded rifle case, gazing at a takedown version of a Swedish Sako PSG90 sniper rifle.

A flicker of hope emerged. He zipped it back up and trotted to the porch.

"Any other firepower in this group?" shouted Payne.

Larkin bolted for his pickup, grabbing a scoped .264 Winchester rifle from the rear seat.

Monroe bent over, retrieving the HK pistol off the dead woman and pulling out three spare magazines and a folding blade. She passed the pistol to Eva. "You used to go hunting with your folks, right?"

She gripped the weapon awkwardly. "Yeah, with a deer rifle, like twenty years ago."

"Thought you were a combat journalist at one time," said Payne.

"Note the latter part of that job title."

He pointed the barrel of her pistol down. "Just direct that towards the target you intend to destroy, and we'll be good."

Payne grabbed Eva's daypack off the porch that the dead woman had brought up with her, sliding Aaron's notebooks and small laptop back inside. He shouldered the Sako rifle and moved to the side of the building. "We need to get some distance between us and those guys, so all of you are going to hoof it north while I stay here for a bit and do some sniping."

"And what about him?" asked Eva, pointing to Wagner.

"I'll handle it," replied Payne, pulling out his newly acquired HK pistol and leveling it at the German's head.

Monroe slapped his arm down. "What the hell are you doing, Payne? You're not going to execute him. He's coming with us."

"Guy like that is not going to end up in jail. Whoever is behind this entire operation has a shitload of cash to throw around. He'll walk, and then all of us will have targets on our backs. I know how this will end."

"How...how do you know?" she asked with narrowed eyes. "Is what he said true: you're a spook?"

Payne licked his lower lip. "Not these days."

"Whatever we're going to do, we'd better do it fast," snapped Larkin, who was poised with his rifle facing towards the main gate.

"Go," shouted Payne.

Monroe returned to the porch and uncuffed Wagner's left hand. She repositioned his hands behind his back while Eva stood over the man with her pistol.

Monroe looked up at the fury in the woman's eyes and slowly moved Eva's arms aside. "He'll get what's coming to him, I promise." She thrust her chin at Gary's lifeless body. "There's been enough killing."

———

Schulz, Regal, and the eight security guards from Wayland finished weaving their way through the pine trees along the west side of the main road.

Schulz raised a fist for the group to pause as he knelt beside a fallen log to scout the field station with his binoculars now that they were within five hundred yards.

Since Wagner hadn't responded to his call, Schulz was on high alert and figured something had gone wrong, so he'd opted for moving in on foot rather than risking the convoy being attacked in the open.

He stopped his sweep when he saw a woman's lifeless body lying beside a large man near the front porch of the building by the drive.

"Damnit, Elke's down."

"What?" asked Regal, settling his AR's rifle scope on the two figures.

"Some shit show," said Fischer, Wayland's security chief. "You fellas got a plan, or we just gonna storm in there and add to the body count?"

Schulz didn't bother pulling away from the binoculars. "Plan is for you to shut the fuck up until I ask you a question. Got it?"

"Whatever. It's your circus. I'm only here because we were told to provide support."

Regal stepped back towards the guy, towering a foot taller than Fischer. He looked into each man's eyes, then down at Fischer. "Your idea of providing support may be a little different than ours. If you can't get on board with taking orders, then haul ass back to your facility. But once we're done here, I'll come and find you. I'll hurt you in ways you can't imagine and chop you up so fine that even the fucking ravens won't be able to find a scrap."

Fischer shuffled back, waving a hand. "Everything's good, Mr. Regal. Anything you need, you got."

Regal glanced down the line at the others, who quickly averted their eyes. The short man with spiky blond hair to Regal's left shrieked as part of his ear and skull blew off, dropping him where he stood.

Regal dropped below the log, crawling towards Schulz. "Where the hell did that come from?"

They heard another thwack, followed by a bearded man beyond Fischer slumping onto his side with half of his jaw missing.

The rest of the guards belly-crawled towards the two Germans and lay motionless.

"Must be the deputy," said Regal.

"Helluva thing to make two clean headshots at this range," said Schulz.

"Or Tommy Larkin," said Fischer. "He's out here all the time. Guy's a cougar hunter."

Schulz and Regal gave each other uneasy glances. "We need to flank this bastard and circle around his back side," said Schulz. He pivoted towards Fischer and his five remaining guards. "Have two of your guards make their way back to the vehicles and charge down the road to that first building. The rest of us will head up this slope and drop down the other side, making our way to the shooter, who must be perched near the largest structure by the driveway."

Fischer nodded, barking orders at the two youngest men in the group, who slunk back into the forest and retraced their steps.

Schulz and Regal crouch-walked for fifty yards until they were clear of the shooter's line of sight, then bounded up the grassy incline. Pausing at the top, Schulz pointed towards a small cabin in the bowl-shaped clearing below.

"You want me to check it out?" asked Fischer.

"Maybe later," said Schulz, who skirted along the rocky ridge for a hundred yards, then proceeded down the slope again. He zigzagged towards the back side of a half-dozen cabins.

Two successive rifle shots rang out.

He dropped and pivoted, seeing Regal and four of the Wayland crew still behind him.

"Looks like a couple more slots just opened up at your facility," Schulz said to the wide-eyed Fischer as both men gazed back towards the still forest near their vehicles.

Schulz turned around, scanning the layout below. He used hand signals to indicate Regal should take two guys and split off to the left while he and the remaining guards would arc to the right and close in upon the shooter.

Schulz kept his AR levelled forward as he and his team began their stalk towards the objective.

AFTER DROPPING the last two men near the vehicles at the gate, Payne retreated, trotting fifty yards behind the dining hall and taking up a shooting perch behind a cluster of empty gas barrels.

He slid out the Sako rifle's mag, confirming there were two of the 7.62x51mm rounds left, then reinserted it. Steadying the barrel on one of the drums, he kept his head back farther than normal from the scope, needing his peripheral vision now.

As suspected, it didn't take long. Three figures were moving around the back of the dining hall, sweeping in towards his last position by the front porch.

Payne watched his quarry and counted down. Finally, he slid his head forward slightly to reacquire the scope sights, welding his cheek against the rifle stock while pacing his breathing.

Five more seconds.

He slid his index finger into position and slowly squeezed the trigger.

The full-metal-jacket round pierced the back end of the bulbous propane tank near the dining hall, delivering a bone-shattering shock wave of flame and shrapnel into the group of armed men.

CHAPTER 34

"What the hell was that?" asked Monroe, glancing back down the trail towards the field station.

"My men barbecuing your colleague," said Wagner, who was trudging along behind Larkin and Kessel.

"Or the other way around is more like it," said Eva. "He's certainly capable of it."

"Because of what you saw at Graves' place?" inquired Monroe.

"It's not what I saw him do as much as the way he did it. It was done with ruthless efficiency, like some of the spec-ops guys I saw overseas when covering wars. Plus, we had an interesting conversation earlier, and let's just say my suspicions about his background were correct."

"Your friend is a killer through and through," said Wagner. "I can spot another wolf when I see one."

"From the little I know of the guy, he seems nothing like you," said Monroe.

The German shrugged his shoulders. "Today, maybe not. Tomorrow, he flips a switch for his particular cause or personal agenda, and he becomes a rabid dog tearing you apart."

"And what's your cause, lining the pockets of the Wayland Corporation?" asked Eva.

"Merely a means to an end. I have other plans." His eyes filled with rage as he glanced back at the journalist. "At least I did until your friend killed my woman."

"He's not my friend, exactly." Eva frowned as she said it, still unsure about Payne's motivations. "Besides, your psycho girlfriend had it coming."

Wagner stopped, turning to face her. "What is he, then? Do you even know the company you keep? Look into his eyes, and you will see the black hole that's in a man like him."

Monroe pushed past Eva, shoving Wagner along the trail. "All I see when I look into your eyes is a sign on the road saying 'Asshole Ahead.' Now, get moving."

A few minutes later, they all paused, hearing footfalls behind them.

Eva breathed a sigh of relief at the sight of Payne trotting up. He was armed only with a pistol and his daypack. "That explosion, was that..." She paused, glancing at a laceration on his forehead from the earlier fight with Wagner.

"The crew that arrived is now half their size or less," said Payne.

"And the others?" asked Monroe.

"We should assume they'll be in pursuit."

"You have no idea what's coming next," said Wagner. "My employer will level this entire valley if necessary."

Payne stepped closer, sending a vicious jab into his solar plexus. "Then yours will be the first grave."

CHAPTER 35

JACOB SCHULZ FORCED HIMSELF TO SIT UP, HIS HEAD AND BACK throbbing like he'd been slammed into a concrete wall. The air around the field station was heavy with smoke and the acrid odor of burnt steel and human flesh.

He didn't know how long he'd been unconscious, but from his rain-soaked clothing, he knew it had been a while. He also knew from the proximity of the blast to Regal's position, his friend had been vaporized in the explosion.

Schulz stood, coughing and rubbing his watery eyes. He glanced at the still form on his right, kicking Fischer in the calf. The Wayland security chief rolled to his side, moaning as he got up on one knee.

The remaining two men on Fischer's team stood, looking like they'd put out a campfire with their faces.

"Fuck happened?" Fischer asked.

"We were set up. This couldn't have been the deputy's handiwork or even that cougar hunter. Wagner said he had another person he was holding. Told me it was a guy who was with Eva Daly. Any ideas on who that could be?"

"Sounds like the person we picked up on our security

cams around our research facility yesterday. Not sure who he is, but he had some moves."

"How so?"

Fischer sliced his open hand through the air. "I mean, he knew how to fight and laid out a few of McG's guys before they took him down."

Schulz glanced at the smoldering heap of metal where the propane tank had been and the two charred corpses in the driveway. He looked at the vehicles down the driveway, then out towards the main gate. "All the rigs are still here. Where could they have gone?"

"Beachum Trail. It's the only other way out of here," said Brad Turco, the assistant security chief. "I used to horseback ride through this property when I was growing up."

"Where's it go?" asked Schulz.

"Intersects Forest Road 334 a little over five miles from here. From there, they could head to one of the small cattle ranches."

"This guy McG you work with, the dope grower, can he be trusted?" asked Schulz.

"His trust is practically guaranteed with him being on our payroll. Plus, he's already got blood on his hands, which we can use for leverage. He and his guys always have sat phones with 'em, so Graves will pick up if you ring him."

Schulz gazed at the dense forest beyond the field station. "I imagine he has to know every hideout and side canyon in these parts." He removed the satellite phone from his vest pocket, examining it for damage, then handed it to Fischer. "These devices are unaffected by the comms blanket we put over the town, so call McG. Double his money for heading off Eva Daly and her little band."

Fischer dialed the number, looking over at Schulz. "How many guys you need him to bring?"

"All of them."

McG GLANCED in his rearview mirror again, pleased that no one was on the road. During the past half hour driving back from Weaverville, where he'd dropped his aunt and uncle, he'd been deep in thought. Between losing Toko and a quarter of this year's crop going up in flames in his barn, he felt like his feet were on the edge of a crumbling cliff.

And it didn't help that Eva Daly and the outsider Payne were on the loose, probably being debriefed by a DEA team in Redding, who were planning a tactical strike on McG's encampments.

So it was with relief that he received the fortuitous call and financial offer from Jacob Schulz on his satellite phone. He pulled over and lowered his truck window for better reception while Fischer relayed the details.

As soon as he'd finished, McG called his second-in-command, Ron Petrie. "Did you already pull back our nearest crews from their sites?"

"All but three, who are held up by the road conditions."

"Twelve guys, good. Have 'em get outfitted with as much ammo and firepower as they can carry, along with their evasion kits."

Petrie returned in a pensive voice, "DEA coming...is a strike imminent?"

"A strike is coming, alright, but we're the ones delivering it. I'll be at your location in half an hour. Then we're going hunting."

WHEN GRAVES finally pulled in at the remote base camp, his men were fully decked out in ballistic vests, backpacks and equipped with AK-47s.

Petrie trotted up to Graves' truck and handed him a set of night-vision goggles and a fresh bottle of water. "Ready to roll when you are," said Petrie.

Graves proceeded to a tree to relieve himself while continuing to relay what he'd been told by Fischer.

"So we're going to take down a couple of cops, too?"

"They know too much about Wayland's operations and about mine."

"What about Hanson...he's going to be all over this once he learns two of his deputies were killed."

"That old fuck is already dead. Fischer said a team connected with Wayland's boss rolled in yesterday and has been cleaning up the mess created by Aaron Daly."

Petrie's face took on an arctic appearance. "God, so the entire sheriff's department is about to be wiped clean off this Earth. This place is going to be swarming with feds after this. We'll lose the chance to harvest all the crops."

McG zipped up his fly. "We'll have to go dark, operate only at night like we did a few years ago when the state task force was cracking down on growers around NorCal. It'll extend the harvest season, but it's the only way." He knew this would probably be the beginning of a larger conflict with the feds, but he was already working on a plan to shift the blame to Fischer and the Wayland Corporation.

Graves marched towards the first outbuilding, which was a twelve-by-twenty shed painted camouflage. He tore down the large map on the wall and headed back outside, placing it on a table beneath the open-air dining area under a flapping canvas tarp. "Gather around. I want all eyes on our travel route."

During the drive back, he had been determining how best to pitch the coming fight and convince his men to assault a group containing two law enforcement officers and three civilians. Or at least two civilians since he wasn't sure what category Payne fell into.

The mass of weathered figures who huddled around him ranged in age from eighteen to forty and were of a variety of ethnic backgrounds. All of the men had beards and rough hands from months of living in the elements.

Graves stabbed his finger at a gulch near the end point of Beachum Trail before it intersected Forest Road 334. "The guy who killed our brothers and my best friend Toko, and torched our barn, is on the run and heading north on the Beachum Trail." He made sure to emphasize the wording of the collective connection to Toko and the barn. "A group of Wayland's security guys are pursuing from the south. We're going to cut off this guy and his buddies from the north, near Rattlesnake Gulch."

He glanced at the tan faces around him. "This fucking animal Payne is a rogue DEA agent from downstate who is running his own Wild West show out here with the local cops. They're planning to take over my operation and rake in all of the profits from your hard work. We're not going to let that happen."

Graves pointed at the map. "My family has worked too hard over the years to create this business. I have worked too hard, and you have all sweated for too long to let some thugs aligned with our corrupt government steal what is ours."

He arched up, putting his hands on his hips. "So if any of you have misgivings about taking down some dirty cops or the rest of Payne's thieving shitbags, then you're welcome to depart right now. No questions asked."

There were a few moments of mumbling between the group, but no one chose to dissent. He knew most of them had nowhere to go, and they were also worried about being shot in the back if they turned tail.

Graves gave a hearty nod, then extended his hand out

towards Petrie, who gave him a scoped AR rifle. "Follow behind me in single file on your dirt bikes so we're not leaving more than one trail of tracks. It's only three miles to Forest Road 334. Once we stash our bikes in the woods, we'll head down the Beachum Trail and set up an ambush site near the gulch." He raised his rifle in the air. "And remember, after today, we are free men, my brothers."

He made sure to leave out the part about there being one of Wayland's operatives in the group, which Fischer had relayed to him.

Everyone in Payne's band needs to get smoked. I'm not taking any chances on him getting away this time.

———

THE RAIN PELTING against Theo Davenport's high-rise office window near downtown LA had increased, which seemed to keep pace with his rising blood pressure. It didn't help that his security chief in Absynth had called, notifying him about the botched attempt by Bana's men to locate Aaron Daly's research files.

His office door opened, and Mikal Bana entered, tossing his rain-dappled trench coat on the leather sofa against the wall and sitting down like he was about to enjoy a movie.

"Any reason you come when you're not asked?" inquired Davenport. "We're not supposed to meet until the handoff of the pathogen."

"My pilot informed me that there is a narrow window of opportunity in this storm to fly north, so I thought *you* can accompany me to your lab."

Davenport leaned forward, steepling his fingers as he stared at the oligarch. "I think you're getting our arrangement confused. I will deliver the product to you. You will then distribute it through your supply chains around Europe. End of story."

Bana picked up a book on Aristotle from the coffee table, smirking before tossing it on the couch. "You spend too much time in this air-conditioned building on your laptop or in your books, contemplating how the world works. When things go to shit with one of your deals, you just move on to another business endeavor like it's nothing."

The former GSG operator leaned forward, shooting a piercing gaze at the CEO. "But once I commit to a deal, it will be completed regardless of the sweat or blood needed to make it happen, and I have too much at stake with my network in Europe to half-ass this operation because your crew in that rat-shit town couldn't handle a simple security issue."

Davenport suddenly felt naked without his personal bodyguard and debated pressing the distress button under his desk. Then he reassured himself that Bana was only venting and wouldn't dare risk biting the hand that was about to feed him.

He cleared his throat, deepening his voice as he replied, "Relax, Mikal. You'll get what we agreed to. Besides, my man Fischer indicated that it was your team of hotshots who screwed the pooch on finding Aaron Daly's incriminating files, and now half of them are dead, and your guy Wagner is a captive."

Bana grated his palms together, then gripped both hands. "He won't be for long. Wagner is one of my best and has a plan buried in his madness. He will come through. And just as a review of recent events, what kind of research facility has such piss-poor security features that Daly even discovered what your researchers were doing out there?"

The German raised an outstretched hand. "Don't bother

answering since we are merely running in circles. This whole thing will soon be resolved, but, in the meantime, I will be flying to Redding on my jet in three hours if the current weather pattern holds. Instruct your staff at the facility outside of Absynth that I will be arriving after that in a cargo helicopter around sunrise to procure the shipment. You can come with me or not."

Davenport stood, heading to the small table near the bookshelves and grabbing two glasses and the brandy tumbler. He clutched everything firmly to prevent his hands from further trembling.

This fucking Neanderthal is telling me the way it is! We'll see about that when we get to my facility.

He set down the glasses on the coffee table and poured two drinks, sliding one towards Bana. "To our safe flight and to a new future, then."

Davenport and the German toasted one another, the CEO trying to muster a predatory gaze like the man across from him.

CHAPTER 36

NINETY MINUTES INTO THE TREK, LARKIN STOPPED UNDER A large oak tree whose massive branches draped over the trail. "Let's take five."

"We should keep pushing on," said Eva.

Larkin thrust his chin towards Kessel, who had slumped to the ground while Monroe inspected his bandages.

"Oh, right," replied Eva.

Payne kicked the backs of Wagner's legs so he collapsed. "You heard the man; take a break."

The German remained on his knees, glancing at Payne and up at the fading light over the treetops. "Soon, you will lose your advantage. Then my men will use their NVGs to pick you apart."

"I think you meant to use the singular term 'man,' since most of your crew are feeding the worms back at that field station. So much for being an elite team."

Wagner smiled. "Surely, you must know how it goes in this line of work. Every day brings a new surprise, sometimes that is the surprised look on the face of the person you were sent to kill, and other days, it's the surprise that occurs when

Murphy's Law rears its head during an op. Either way, one learns to be fluid and adapt."

"Or die."

Wagner chuckled. "Yes, that too."

After Monroe finished helping Kessel, she moved up closer to Payne. "So, is what Eva told me true...you were with some kind of clandestine agency at one time?"

Payne flared an eyebrow, looking at the deputy. "Not the time or place or appropriate audience."

She huffed out an exhale, glancing between both men, then departing and heading up to Larkin.

"Ah, the toll of a life of secrets, my friend," said Wagner.

Except I'm done with that life.

He gazed over at Eva, whose look of anguish had only increased since he met her, knowing he would always have this shadow-self whose past he could never fully reveal. He wondered if it was the real reason he was on an extended road trip without an end date. Was it really to explore America and unwind after so many years in the covert-ops world?

Or is it to avoid having to open up to someone else?

Payne shuffled back a few feet, alternating his attention between the German and the two deputies. "How's that shoulder wound look?"

"The bleeding has slowed, but he needs to get to a hospital," Larkin replied.

"And a shot of morphine would sure be nice," said Kessel, who had a permanent wince on his pale face.

Larkin moved off into the brush, returning a minute later with a handful of twigs. He trimmed them down to pencil length and handed the batch to Kessel. "Chew on that, son. Willow has salicin in the bark and has been used for pain for thousands of years around the world."

"Really?" asked Monroe.

The old cougar hunter nodded. "That was the primary ingredient in Bayer aspirin until the 1940s when industrial medicine began to dominate. I use it all the time for my arthritis. Well, that and a shot of tequila."

"Tommy Larkin, cougar tracker and amateur pharmacist...who knew?" said Monroe. She gave Payne a hard stare. "Everyone in this group is just full of fucking surprises, it seems."

Payne glanced at Larkin's weathered rifle. "That's a beauty."

Larkin ran his thumb under the weapon's shoulder strap. "Yeah, reliable as hell and been in my family a long time."

"Is that what you used for dropping cougars that had become maneaters?"

The older man nodded. "Good for big game of all sizes."

"How much farther to that road?" inquired Monroe.

Larkin and Eva both swapped uneasy glances before he replied, "About two and a half miles, but we'll need to get across Rattlesnake Gulch first."

"Sounds like a fun place," quipped Kessel, who was chewing on a willow sprig.

"Has that old footbridge been upgraded?" asked Eva.

Larkin gritted his teeth together. "Guess we're about to find out."

———

AFTER THE FIRST MILE, Schulz paused on the trail, scanning the boot tracks again for any signs of deviation that someone had stepped off and was planning to ambush them.

He figured the motley crew ahead wouldn't bother since he'd seen blood droplets early on and figured someone in the party was wounded.

Wagner, probably. That's the only way he could've been subdued.

His satellite phone vibrated, and he saw it was Graves' number.

He pulled it from his vest and extended the folding antenna. "Go ahead."

"We're about two hours out from the gulch and will be in position soon. The darkness and the rain are going to make accurate ID of our targets difficult."

"Then get closer or wait until you have fucking accurate ID. I want my commander in one piece, or the cash going into your pocket will be cut in half."

"Roger that."

"Besides getting my commander back, I want Daly's files, and Eva is supposed to have those in her possession. So don't start tossing bodies into the canyon until you've located them."

"I'll see to it. After that, all I care about is this guy Payne. He's cost me a lot, and I have plans for him back at my camp."

"Then we're good. I'll call you again when we are closer to that gulch." Schulz tucked away the phone, gazing back at Fischer and the two other Wayland guys. This day had turned out a lot differently than he expected.

He thought of the loss of Elke and Regal. The former was sure to take a psychological toll on Wagner. Schulz understood the physical attraction his commander had to the woman, but a part of him was relieved she was dead. That would mean a new recruit who was, hopefully, less twisted.

While Schulz understood the occasional use of torture and interrogation to obtain the necessary results, he abhorred the way Elke used it as a first resort to satisfy her lust for controlling others. And Wagner just enabled it as some kind of voyeuristic pleasure.

Schulz had considered not informing Graves that his boss was a captive in the group, but he had no interest, at present, in taking command of Bana's crew of henchmen. He still had much to learn from Wagner, but Schulz also knew that the day would come when he would outgrow his mentor, just as he was sure Wagner was thinking the same thing of his own employer.

———

"EVERYTHING GOOD?" asked Petrie as he stood beside his boss, both of them returning to glassing the field ahead with their binoculars.

"Yeah, just fine." Graves clenched his jaw. "Fuck, no, it's not, actually. There's a small hiccup. I didn't tell the men earlier, but there's a guy in the group we're about to hit who needs to be spared. Some fucking German dude who works for Wayland. He's a big deal, I guess."

Petrie glanced up at the gray sky. "That's going to mean getting closer than we wanted. Could be an issue for some of our crew. Sniping some dudes from a few hundred yards is one thing, but seeing their faces in your scope before pulling the trigger is another, especially if they see the cops in uniform. Not all of 'em will be able to do that, trust me."

"That's why I'm bringing it up now. You saw action over in Afghanistan, so I know it won't be a problem for you and some of the other guys, but I don't need half our crew turning and running, especially when they see that two of the faces are women."

Petrie glanced down the line of men hunched in the brush on either side. "It'll be dark soon, so that'll help. And if any of our guys do split, I'll go after them."

"Thanks, brother. You know you and Toko have been the

only two solid dudes I could rely on all these years. You've always had my back, and you're like family to me."

"Means a lot, boss. I feel the same way."

Graves just needed to hold the leash on his men a little longer. Once this was over and he got his payday from Wayland, he could easily buy twice as many parcels of land around Absynth and further expand his empire, which would make up for this year's crop loss within twenty-four months.

And it's my word against Eva's that I killed her brother. There is no actual proof...unless Fischer has some video footage I don't know about. Shit, does he?

He chewed on his lip, chiding himself for admitting such a dumb-ass thing to Eva.

This whole thing's a fucking mess. Just get this current job out of the way and then figure out the rest tomorrow. You'll get through this like always...and come out rich as hell.

He repeated the last sentence a few times until the sour taste in his mouth began to dissipate.

CHAPTER 37

PAYNE CLIMBED DOWN FROM THE LARGE PINE TREE OVERLOOKING the meadow to the south that they had crossed a half hour earlier. The last trickle of sunlight penetrating the hazy gray skies had just faded, and they would be doing the last half of this trek in the dark.

"Looks like there's four guys on our tail after all," he said.

"I told you," said Wagner. "My people would walk through a storm of daggers for me."

"You mean the idiot at the front. The other three are wearing security guard uniforms, so I guess you're down to your last man."

Wagner turned his gaze towards the forest.

"How far out are they?" asked Monroe.

"Thirty minutes, maybe forty-five at best," said Payne. "They still have to hike up the switchbacks we just did in getting to this spot, so that will slow them down a bit."

Kessel adjusted his shoulder sling slightly, glancing at Larkin. "Can't you just use your knowledge of mountain lions and lead these scumbags to a place where they'll get eaten?"

Larkin smirked, his caterpillar-like mustache twisting. "That ain't how it works, son. Cougars aren't elk...they don't travel in herds, and they sure as hell aren't predictable. And in an area like this, one male cougar has a range of a hundred and fifty square miles."

"Maybe we can save the natural history lesson for later," said Eva. "What are we going to do now?"

Larkin thrust his bristly chin up the trail. "It's about fifteen minutes to the gulch; then we all gotta get across that bridge, which will eat up another twenty minutes since it'll be best to go one at a time."

"Any way to drop that bridge once we're across?" asked Payne.

The old hunter shook his head. "Doubtful. It's a cable suspension bridge; the anchors are bolted into the bedrock on each side of the canyon."

Payne gazed back towards the meadow. "Then we need to slow them down here so everyone can get across without being sniped."

He removed his daypack, unzipping the main compartment and removing a Bic lighter and a box of waterproof matches from his survival kit along with a small container of cotton balls smeared with Vaseline.

"Eva and I will stay here for a few minutes while the rest of you make for that bridge." He looked at Larkin. "Once everyone's on the other side of the gulch, find a perch so you can cover us with your rifle, 'cause we're probably gonna be sprinting across."

"You may rethink that last part when you see the bridge," said Eva.

"Go, while you still have time," Payne said.

Larkin, Wagner and the two deputies resumed their trek north while Eva followed Payne down the trail in the opposite direction.

A hundred yards later, he stopped, pointing to the dead plant stalks along the trail. "These are all milkweed plants." He grabbed a thumb-sized brown pod and crushed it, releasing clusters of downy seed heads. "Fill your pockets with as many as you can while I gather some pine sap and branches."

"But everything's soaked."

"Exactly why I need the pine sap. It'll burn like kerosene regardless of the weather. Weren't you in the Girl Scouts, or do any survival training when you were growing up out here?"

"I think your experiences in the outdoors, and life in general, were far, far different than mine, Payne."

"Fair enough." He walked into the woods, using his folding knife to pry off gobs of crystallized pine sap from the bark of the mature trees. After he had filled his back pocket, he began gathering finger-thick branches and fine twigs from the dead standing evergreens, which would contain less moisture than anything on the ground and have the added benefit of being laced with trace amounts of sap, making ignition in the rain easier. Lastly, he peeled off some of the rotten bark, shoving it under his arm.

Payne returned to the trail, squatting between a cluster of large boulders on either side. He placed a single bark slab on the wet ground, followed by a handful of pine sap clumps. Next, he added a tuft of milkweed down, then constructed a mini tipi structure over the top and used a match to light the seed heads.

The flame lingered long enough to ignite the pine sap, which fizzled and spread quickly, catching the twigs on fire. Lastly, he placed a handful of the thicker branches over this.

"You go gather handfuls of green pine needles while I get this fire built up."

"Why, what's the point?"

"Stop being a damn journalist needing to know everything and get as many bundles of pine needles as you can carry. You'll learn why soon enough."

A few minutes later, the flames were knee-high, and he laid on the remaining branches. Once Eva returned, they began piling on the tufts of green pine needles. Payne stepped off the trail and grabbed some handfuls of dead bracken ferns and added them to the fire.

The orange flames quickly turned to billowing plumes of gray smoke, causing both of them to step back.

He pointed towards the rim where the trail descended towards the meadow. "The low pressure system of this storm is going to keep this smoke close to the ground, and it's going to choke this area, reducing visibility. It's the same thing as using a smoke grenade...it'll obscure the vision of the guys below and slow their pace because they'll be expecting an ambush."

"You sound pretty confident."

"I've been on the receiving end before. You don't rush blindly into a chokepoint, or you risk getting picked apart by booby traps or a sniper staked out on an angle to the approach route."

When they'd finished, he motioned her to follow as they ran up the trail in the direction of the gulch. Payne paused by the pine tree he'd first climbed to scout the meadow. He gazed back at the billowing clouds of gray smoke that were floating through the forest and descending below.

––––––––

ONCE THE SMOKE from the fires floated over the trail, Payne left Eva behind a large tree trunk, handing her two orange glow sticks from his daypack.

He slipped into the forest and circled down to the left,

walking parallel to the trail. With night-time cloaking the landscape, he paused to remove the headlamp from his daypack, flicking on the red-light option before continuing.

Thirty feet later, Payne squatted, listening for sounds of movement now that the rain had died down. The damp leaves were going to be a disadvantage since he wouldn't hear the other party approaching, but he knew once they encountered the smoldering fire, their attention would be focused on their immediate surroundings.

He flicked off his headlamp and focused on the shadows near the orange haze of the remaining campfire coals. A short time later, Payne picked out a slight silhouette of an armed man in the smoke. After a few seconds, he observed another figure, followed by two more.

Payne zeroed in on the last man and slowly made his way through the brush. He had selected this side of the trail to make his assault since it was comprised largely of car-sized boulders and a leafy substrate compared with the downed trees on the other side.

He paused near the last boulder beside the trail. Once the last figure had passed, Payne swept out behind and sank his blade into the man's neck while reaching around the other side and cupping the guy's mouth. He yanked the thrashing figure behind the boulder, slamming his forehead into the rock, then lowering him to the ground.

Payne retrieved the man's suppressed rifle and peered through the night-vision scope at the other figures ahead. He leaned out from the boulder and sent two rounds into the back of the next figure, then placed the green dot of the scope on the head of the second man in line, firing off another round.

Payne quickly ducked around the other side of the boulder and scurried fifteen feet over to a globular rock formation, where he knelt and focused his rifle scope on the direction of where the lead man had last been.

From what he recalled earlier when he had been watching the guys cross the meadow, the first in line was one of Wagner's mercs since the other three were wearing security guard uniforms. Unlike the three Wayland men, though, this merc was no stranger to hunting at night.

But Payne didn't have time for a game of cat and mouse. He picked up a rock and tossed it in the direction of Eva's location, which was as much to distract the merc as it was to alert Eva to her role.

Two orange glow sticks were hurled into the air, landing on the trail.

Payne caught a sliver of movement in the gray smoke beyond the dwindling fire. He squeezed off two rounds in succession, hearing one strike a tree and another one resound with a thump.

The merc stumbled and fell to one knee, trying to swing his rifle up in Eva's direction.

Payne fired off two more rounds, striking the figure in the neck and right ear.

Payne rose from his position and walked back to the location of the first man he had dispatched. Then he walked up the trail, looking for signs of movement in any of the other figures, but the 5.56 rifle rounds had done their job.

He moved up the trail towards Wagner's dead henchman and whispered Eva's name, telling her to come down.

"You all right?" he asked her.

She just nodded, glancing apprehensively at the line of splayed bodies in the eerie gray hue cloaking the trail.

Payne bent over, retrieving the tactical vest off the dead merc. He inspected the six rifle magazines, two frag grenades, and satellite phone, then slid it over his chest.

After he gathered the gear he needed and was ready to

depart, the satellite phone vibrated. He and Eva gave each other pensive glances.

Payne pulled out the phone and answered.

"Me and my guys are at the bridge. How far out are you?" Matt Graves' voice sent an icy chill down Payne's neck. It was a move he hadn't anticipated, and now Monroe and the others were heading right into the thug's hands.

Payne stared at Eva and raised a finger to his lips as he thought about his next move. He pulled the collar of his shirt over his mouth and held the phone back a few inches farther from his face. "Ten minutes away."

"Once they get across the bridge and I can confirm that Eva has her brother's research materials, we'll eliminate them and toss their bodies in the gulch. Everyone but Payne; I want him alive."

Eva held a hand up to her mouth.

Payne rested a hand on her shoulder while he responded, "Copy that, be at your six shortly." He folded down the antenna on the phone and slid it back into his vest.

"God, we have to warn them," said Eva.

"There's no way we can get to them in time, and Graves probably has twenty guys staked out along the gulch, but I have an idea that might turn things to our advantage."

CHAPTER 38

"We're leveling off. I'll try to keep the air pockets to a minimum," said Bana's pilot over the speakers in the G7 jet as Davenport and the German oligarch glanced below at the LA skyline.

At the far end of the cabin was Tyrell, Davenport's bodyguard, who nearly occupied both seats with his muscular girth, but he seemed a mile away from Davenport's perspective.

"You should try the caviar; it comes straight from the sea not far from our estate back home," said Alina Bana, who sat beside her husband, her black hair up in a tight bun.

Davenport found himself having to forcefully avert his eyes from her alluring figure in a blue satin dress that hugged her luscious frame. "I'll be fine, thank you. This will probably be a very turbulent flight, after all."

Bana gave him a dismissive look, leaning his head back and closing his eyes.

Yeah, you used to be a badass in special ops, jumping out of fucking planes in the middle of the night, you pompous piece of shit. Well, I turned my empire in the US into a billion-dollar industry and have crushed countless rivals to get where I'm at today, so piss off.

He emitted a plastic smile at Alina. "So nice to finally meet you. I had hoped we would have done so earlier, but it seemed like it was always about business."

"Yes, Mikal has told me of your meetings." She sent him a piercing gaze, resting her fingers with the glossy red nails upon her husband's forearm. "But he only makes a move on something if he is one hundred percent certain of its outcome and profitability, which is how I know our joint venture will benefit us all."

You dumb bitch...you talk like you're an astute businesswoman when you're nothing but arm candy. He gazed at her diminutive diamond ring.

She noticed his look and leaned forward, resting her hand on his knee. "I told Mikal such jewelry was not important to me, and I only wanted something small." She leaned back, removing one of the long golden hairpins from her bun. "This has far more value and was the real wedding gift I requested." She handed it to him.

Davenport marveled at the slender shape, the entire eight-inch tapered length made of solid gold. Along the sides was the finely etched image of a dragon raining fire down upon a man who was running away. He held it closer, examining what looked like a trace of blood.

"That's a rare piece from the Ming dynasty. It belonged to the wife of a wealthy silk merchant. Legend has it that she killed many of her husband's business rivals in their sleep. Then, one day, she discovered that her husband's own brother had betrayed them. So she poisoned him with a single prick from that. Slowly, over the course of a month, his insides turned to liquid. Or so the tale goes."

A vein in Davenport's neck bulged, and he quickly handed it back to her. "Fascinating heirloom."

"I find the traditional stories of old that were born out of trust and betrayal, and integrity and dishonor, to be so fascinating." She slid the hairpin carefully back into place while letting her eyes linger on him. "Don't you agree, Mr. Davenport?"

He nodded. "Quite so."

Davenport stood, forcing his shoulders back. "Excuse me. I need to talk with my man about some upcoming logistics." He headed towards his bodyguard, removing a handkerchief from his pocket and dabbing his damp forehead.

CHAPTER 39

Monroe kept her flashlight focused on Wagner as he crossed the bridge and joined Larkin and Kessel on the other side. Before departing, she readjusted his handcuffs, placing them in front to make his passage easier, but a part of her wished he would take a tumble onto the rocks a hundred feet below.

Such justice would be poetic, especially after what Wagner had done to Hanson and Gary. *Certainly, Payne wouldn't fret.*

She thought about his unbridled willingness to kill Wagner earlier. Monroe had almost held her tongue then. She knew Hanson would probably have looked the other way while Payne pulled the trigger. She wrestled with reconciling the Old West values of her mentor with what was expected of her as a modern law enforcement officer.

Monroe had no moral qualms about seeing someone like Wagner buried in a shallow grave in the backcountry, but it didn't sit well with the symbol of order and justice she and her department were supposed to stand for.

Once Wagner was across the gulch, Monroe holstered her service pistol and took a deep breath, moving onto the cable bridge, steadying herself on the pressure-treated wooden planks that spanned the two-foot width. Larkin kept the pathway illuminated with his flashlight while she took baby steps along the creaky bridge.

It wasn't until Monroe was at the midpoint that she noticed it. Her peripheral vision caught a momentary flutter of what she thought were fireflies behind Larkin and the others. She paused, sucking in a deep breath of damp air, and blinked hard, seeing it was a dozen flashlights sweeping towards the gulch.

"Shit, look out," she yelled, gripping the cable handrails on either side while watching a dozen armed men emerge from the forest.

Given the torrential rain, Larkin and Kessel were oblivious until it was too late.

The hulking figure of Matt Graves stood out from the new arrivals as his men swept in and disarmed Larkin and Kessel.

Graves walked to the mouth of the bridge, shouting, "It's over, Monroe. Now, take out your pistol and drop it over the side."

She clutched the cable handrail tighter, wanting to bolt across and strangle the man. Instead, she leaned back with one hand and did as he instructed, then finished her walk to the other side.

"The handcuff keys are in her coat pocket," said Wagner as he held his arms towards Graves.

The dope kingpin uncuffed the German, who gave Graves a stern look. "Eva Daly and Payne were lagging behind. Her brother's laptop and notebooks are in Payne's backpack. Tell my man Schulz to destroy everything." He glanced at the inky tree line. "I need a ride to the Wayland site to get the shipment ready for the coming flight."

"Sure thing," said Graves.

"So it's true. You're Wayland's lapdog," Monroe said to Graves.

"You know, I thought you'd be smarter, Becky," Graves said. "But like your boss, who'd never take a bribe, you're too stuck in a black-and-white world, and that's not how things work anymore."

"Anything to ease your conscience," she said. Monroe shot a glance beyond Graves, seeing Larkin tensing up like he was going to bolt forward and attack the man. She shook her head and was relieved to see Larkin get the message.

Graves waved the barrel of his AK, motioning her to walk over and stand between Larkin and Kessel. Graves obviously noticed the cougar hunter balling his fists because he pointed the rifle at his chest. "Why am I not surprised you're here. You always were the big papa bear to the Monroes."

Larkin sent a fierce gaze at Graves. "I had sure hoped to run into you in the backwoods under different circumstances than these."

Graves chuckled. "You got some fire in your belly, old-timer."

"Enough squabbling," said Wagner. He extended his hand, nodding at the Glock 17 in a leg holster on Graves' side.

The dope dealer slid it out, passing the firearm to him.

"Where is your transportation?" Wagner asked.

Graves glanced over at Petrie. "Take him back to the bikes and get him over to the Wayland place."

His second-in-command motioned for two guys to accompany him.

Wagner paused before Monroe. "Shame I won't be here when your friend Payne gets mowed down, but I have a bird to catch, and the sooner I can get out of this country, the better."

———

FIFTEEN MINUTES after Wagner and Petrie departed, one of Graves' guys whistled.

With all of their flashlights turned off, Graves had to strain his eyes to make out movement on the bridge.

He flicked on his flashlight but then immediately lowered his rifle when he saw two Wayland security guards crossing in hooded rain jackets. They moved slowly, their bodies swaying with each blast of wind. Graves' eyes settled on the bulbous backpack the thin man at the rear was carrying, but his shoulders slumped, knowing that someone else had put a bullet in Payne.

———

"REMEMBER, keep your head down and just hand off the pack to Graves. I'll handle the rest," whispered Payne as they crossed the halfway point on the bridge.

"You sure this is gonna work?" Eva asked.

"Certainty rarely figures into this sorta thing."

"That's reassuring."

———

GRAVES EMERGED from the stand of young pines as his men did the same. He leaned to his right, yelling above the fierce rain at a tall guy named Bledsoe, only a few feet away. "Once I get Aaron Daly's stuff, take Monroe and the others to the edge of the gulch and have these Wayland guards do the dirty work. No need to have the blood of two LEOs on our hands."

"You got it," said Bledsoe.

The lead Wayland guard stepped off the bridge and

approached, raising his outstretched palm for Graves to lower his flashlight farther while the rain pounded at his nylon hoodie.

"Sorry, man, didn't mean to blind you."

The thin security guard paused a few feet away, lowering the backpack on the ground. The rain was coming down in sheets so thick that it was impossible to see more than ten feet.

Graves was about to speak when the lead security guy rushed forward with his rifle aimed at Monroe. "This bitch needs to die. I lost a lot of my friends because of her."

Graves gave Bledsoe a pleasing look before shouting at the back of the guard, "Do it by the rim of the gulch."

The two guards waved the barrel at Monroe's face, directing her and the rest of her group to the cliff.

Bledsoe retrieved the backpack and handed it to his boss. Graves slung his rifle, unclipping the two latches and flipping back the top as Bledsoe shone his light inside at a thick nest of pine needles surrounding two live grenades.

Graves' mouth twisted as he looked at the pins tethered by a piece of string to the bag's latches.

———

THIRTY FEET AWAY, Payne lifted the hood on his rain jacket and removed two Sig Sauer pistols, handing one to Monroe and another to Kessel while Eva handed over her AR rifle to Larkin.

Payne swept his rifle-mounted flashlight to a fallen log. "Take cover, now!"

He leaped over the log, dropping down on the other side as the rest of the group mimicked his actions.

The explosion rattled the air and sent a shock wave

through the trees. It was followed by the screams of numerous men.

Payne hopped up, flicking his rifle light back on and shooting two dazed figures near where Graves had been standing. He swept his weapon to the right, zippering the torsos of two guys leaning over their downed friends.

While Payne continued his target elimination, Larkin joined in, dropping two goons near the bridge. Payne heard the deputies' pistols barking out beside him.

A few seconds later, the shooting ceased. The air was filled with the sickening smell of charred flesh and burnt wood.

Payne darted towards a large pine tree and arced his way towards where Graves' crew had been situated. One man was crawling on his belly towards his rifle, and Payne squeezed off a round into the guy's head. He swept his light over the area, seeing twelve bullet-riddled bodies splayed along the forest floor.

Graves was on his back, his right ear and jaw shredded. The man's chest was barely rising as a bronchial sound emanated from his mouth.

The shot of a rifle startled Payne, and he swung his barrel to the right as Larkin approached. The man fired two more rounds into Graves' chest and one in his forehead.

Payne looked into the rabid gaze of the old cougar hunter, who turned away and leaned a trembling hand against a tree.

"Damn, Tommy. You alright?" asked Payne.

"Never better."

Payne noticed a strange look on Monroe's face, wondering how the law enforcement officer in her was processing Larkin's murderous rage along with all of their recent actions.

"Is it over?" asked Eva, who came up beside Payne.

"Almost." He thrust his chin back towards the opposite side. "We'll have to return another time for your brother's laptop and notes."

"Wagner left with a couple of Graves' guys for the agro-site," said Monroe, surveying the carnage.

Payne glanced up at the sky, which had lessened its rainfall. "They're gonna have to move the pathogen out of that facility fast and will use any opening they can get in this storm."

He leaned over one of the dead bodies and removed the GPS in the vest. Payne activated it and sifted through the most recent waypoints. "This must lead back to their dirt bikes."

"Just get us there, and I can do the rest," said Eva.

Kessel and Monroe retrieved AKs from the ground and followed Payne through the forest, all of them glancing back occasionally at the gulch-side graveyard.

———

"WHICH WAY TO WAYLAND'S FACILITY?" Payne asked, getting onto the bike and slinging his rifle across his back.

"About twelve miles southwest, but it's a tangle of roads to get there."

Eva and Monroe both mounted bikes beside him. "I know the way," Eva said, kick-starting the Yamasaki like it was her own.

"And three guns are better than two," said Monroe.

"So your safety is off now. What happened to upholding the law?" asked Payne.

"I plan to uphold it however I can. But I have no problem if Wagner meets a different fate than going to prison."

Payne glanced into the eyes of each woman. "I'm not complaining. I just want to make sure both of you realize what we're walking into at that lab. If we're going to prevent that pathogen from leaving these shores, then the gloves have to come off. This is going to get a lot uglier."

Monroe and Eva gave each other nervous glances. "We're wasting time," said Monroe.

Eva tied her hair back in a tight ponytail, then revved the throttle and took off down the road.

Payne motioned for Monroe to go next. He glanced over at Larkin and Kessel hunkered down beside an overturned tree root.

Payne removed the satellite phone from his vest and drove it over to them. "Maybe you can get through to one of the ranches out here that you mentioned. And once you do, have them contact the FBI office in Redding. Just tell them to expect a small war at that Wayland facility."

CHAPTER 40

AFTER FORTY MINUTES OF DRIVING ON THE SLICK MUDDY ROAD, Eva stopped for the third time to gaze down a spur trail on the left. She turned the front wheel so the headlight shone down the pathway as she stared up at the larger trees lining the route.

"Are you sure you know the way?" shouted Payne above the rainfall pelting them.

There was a pregnant pause as Eva retraced her eyes along the trees, then glanced down at the ground. "Yeah, this is the turnoff we need."

Payne shot a worried glance at Monroe. "You don't sound convincing," he said. "We don't have time to backtrack if you're wrong."

"I'm sure. It took me a minute, but I recognize these redwoods. They're the only ones on this side of the valley. Aaron and I used to ride our horses this way to get to my granddad's place."

"The Wayland site...that was your family's at one time, too?" said Monroe. "Geez, I knew you guys were spread all over the countryside but didn't know it extended this far out."

"All I remember is that it was sold when I was twelve to some company out of LA. If only I could go back in time and warn my grandfather about what Wayland had in store."

"That company would have just found another site in another lonely pocket of the state to conduct its research," said Payne.

Eva wiped the grit off her cheeks, then nodded towards the trail. "Give each other some space, this is going to be tight, and there's probably a shitload of big roots along the trail, so go slow. Unless anything's changed, it should take us about twenty minutes to reach the northeast corner of the property."

"What happens after that?" asked Monroe.

"I have an idea, but won't know if it's viable until I see the property again." She glanced at Payne. "After that, you're center stage, Mr. Secret Agent."

————

By THE TIME they arrived at the edge of the property, Payne and the two women had a flurry of facial lacerations from skirting between miles of branches lining the trail.

Eva paused at the edge of the tree line, pointing to a large rectangular patch of unkempt grass to the right. It was surrounded by rusty, eight-foot-high fencing, which extended a half mile to the west before sloping down towards the main buildings at the other end of the property near the main entrance of the eighty-acre holding.

"This doesn't look like it was ever cultivated for wheat," he said, pulling back the hood on his rain jacket as the storm abated and the subtle hint of dawn emerged.

"Too rocky and not very good drainage this far up, so it

looks like they've never done anything with it," Eva said. "Same issues my great-grandfather had, which is why he left it feral."

Payne removed the binoculars that he had lifted off one of the dead men by the gulch. He scanned the terrain ahead all the way up to the two-story structure, barns and outbuildings a quarter mile away. The misty haze made it difficult to see, and he had to strain his eyes to discern the layout.

"They're going to see us coming once this fog clears, if their cameras haven't spotted us already," said Monroe, who dismounted and was kneeling in the shrubs.

"We should be good." He pointed to a newer section of the fence that was five hundred yards away and ran parallel to the old fence line beside them. "The few cameras they have are on that newer segment down below. And those models usually have a range of about twenty yards."

Eva got off her bike, letting it fall on its side. She pointed to a small berm just a few feet away on the other side of the fence, which had a vertical vent sticking four feet out of the dirt. "That's our way in, assuming it's still intact."

"Is that a septic mound?" asked Monroe.

"No, air shaft. You might remember the rumors about my great-granddad being a rum-runner during the Prohibition Days...well, this was the tunnel he used for smuggling things in and out when he knew the cops were watching the main house. Aaron and I used to play in those."

"What's on the other end?" asked Payne. "If we manage to get down into the passage and make it to the facility, how do we know that the original entrance hasn't been filled with concrete?"

"Look, I don't have all the answers." Eva shrugged. "But I don't think we have a lot of options. If we charge ahead towards the front entrance, Wagner is going to see us coming."

Payne raised his hand, waving at them to be quiet. His eyes darted along the treetops to the south as the familiar sound of a roaring engine grew evident. "Helo, a large one. Probably dual rotors."

A few seconds later, a cargo helicopter descended in the parking lot adjacent to the main facility.

"That'd be Wagner's boss coming for his payload. Once that bird is loaded and takes off, they'll be out of our reach and Europe can kiss its economy goodbye."

The sound of voices penetrated the fog, and several bobbing flashlights became evident along the pathway skirting the fence line to the south.

"Shit, they must have heard our bikes when we arrived," said Eva.

"Or they're just doing a standard security sweep," said Monroe.

"Follow me." Payne returned to the Yamasakis as the women did the same. They walked the dirt bikes down into a ravine to the left and leaned them against a steep embankment choked with saplings.

―――――

EVA FROZE at the sound of boots crunching along the gravel path above them. She pressed herself against the wet embankment and clutched a thick tree root for stability, feeling Monroe tense beside her.

Payne raised a single finger to his lips as all of them remained motionless. Through the mist, flashes of tactical lights swept the ridgeline twenty feet above. Eva counted four beams, meaning at least that many guards.

"Team One, check in," crackled a voice over a radio.

"Northeast perimeter clear so far," came the response. "We're about to double back."

Eva started to shift position, but Payne gripped her arm, shaking his head. His eyes tracked something Eva couldn't see. Following his gaze, she noticed a stream of pebbles tumbling down the embankment, one of the guards was moving to a position directly above them.

A beam of light cut through the thick branches just inches from her face. Eva held her breath as the guard trampled over the leaf-strewn path overhead. Mud and water dripped onto her neck as the man shifted position.

"Got movement in the tree line," one of the guards called out.

Eva's heart hammered against her ribs. The guy above them turned, his boot dislodging a chunk of mud that slid past her shoulder. She pressed herself flatter against the bank, feeling every muscle trembling with the effort to remain still.

"Check it out," the radio squawked. "The rest of you search the area."

Two of the lights swung away, moving toward the trees.

Eva's lungs burned, and she sensed Monroe beside her, coiled like a spring.

Payne's face was unreadable, but his body language radiated calm focus. He'd probably done this a hundred times in places much worse than northern California, which both reassured and unsettled her.

After what felt like hours, the radio crackled again. "Just a couple of mule deer."

The boots overhead retreated, and the flashlights faded. Still, Payne kept them motionless for another full minute before finally indicating they should move.

Eva released her breath in a quiet rush, her arms shaking as she relaxed her death grip on the tree root.

"That was more than a little nerve-racking," Monroe whispered, brushing wet leaves from her jacket.

"It's about to get a lot worse," Payne replied softly. "If

they follow a standard patrol pattern, then they'll arc out farther during their next sweep, and they might discover our bike tracks in the mud. We need to get into that tunnel while we can."

Eva nodded, trying to still her trembling hands as they prepared to move back towards the gap in the fence.

———

DAVENPORT LED the way through his research facility, serving as a guide for Mikal Bana as they walked past the offices on the main level towards the stairwell leading to the retrofitted basement, where the two laboratories were located.

He was concerned since Fischer hadn't checked in following his last report four hours ago, and he hoped the man was merely occupied with tying up the loose ends with Eva Daly and her pathetic band of locals.

So it was with great surprise that he saw Karl Wagner sitting on a chair near the second lab's observation windows.

Wagner stood and updated his boss on the events in Absynth since their arrival.

"You killed a fucking sheriff?" snapped Davenport. "Are you insane?" The CEO shot a glance at Bana. "When I said I wanted you to handle some of this operation, I didn't mean whacking the local head of law enforcement."

"Relax, Theo. My people are professionals and don't officially exist in any databases, so this will never be traced back to any of us."

Davenport's left eye twitched. He alternated his gaze between each man, then turned and trudged down the hallway.

———

BANA GLANCED around the spacious basement, which had been turned into a small warehouse filled with pallets of scientific supplies. "Where's the rest of the crew?"

Wagner sighed, rubbing the back of his neck. "Elke is gone. Schulz and Regal should be checking in soon. They were mopping up things out at the site I just came from where Eva Daly was at."

"Shame about Elke." He put his hand on Wagner's shoulder, turning towards the large bay windows in the laboratory, where three workers in white hazmat suits were placing the last of two hundred glass tubes containing beetles into padded crates. "It may not seem like it now, but those creatures are going to be the temporary foot soldiers that will put all of Europe in our hands."

Bana glanced over the weary, mud-streaked face of his second-in-command. "We will get past the losses of this week, my friend. Next month at this time, when Europe's food crops are decimated, we will be the rulers of a new empire of our making."

Wagner gave a weak nod. "Almost sounds too easy. I just hope this has been worth it."

Bana turned squarely towards Wagner. "What about commanding all of my holdings in Eastern Europe and making my estate in Bulgaria yours to do with what you wish. Does that make this sound 'worth it'?"

———

THE PUNGENT AIR in the narrow tunnel that greeted Payne was a blend of mold and putrid earth as he lowered himself four feet down to the cobblestone floor.

He shone his rifle's barrel-mounted flashlight past Eva but only saw an inky curtain of uncertainty at the far end.

Payne removed a handheld Surefire flashlight and handed it to Eva. "Let the tour begin."

"Not much to see, though I carved my name in one of the overhead beams a long time ago."

He glanced at the ceiling, which was made of creosote-soaked railroad ties suspended on upright beams of similar material. "This place was built to last."

They crouch-walked in unison, pausing to smash the occasional foot-long centipedes wriggling onto their legs.

"There'd better be a payoff at the end, 'cause I really have no desire to walk back through this again," said Monroe, whose face had lost its color after the third centipede encounter.

Five minutes later, they paused, their necks and backs cramped from the narrowing passage. The ground had dried due to a slight uprise in the passageway floor, and they each leaned against the walls and stretched out their legs.

Only the sound of their breathing was evident, and Payne rested his head back for a moment, sighing and debating his next words. "The seventh floor of Langley called the shots for me for almost fifteen years. During that time, I worked in over sixty countries. The risk-management-consultant story was a convenient cover, though some of my duties entailed keeping diplomats safe when they were abroad."

Eva and Monroe gazed at one another before the deputy spoke. "And you're on leave now, or were you let go?"

"A little of both, I guess. I'm on permanent leave after letting go of the agency. Some things went down on my last mission overseas that were the result of overt negligence at Langley and the greed of the suits in charge. I'd been wanting out for a while and saw the writing on the wall. I figured a road trip up the coast for a few months…or few years was a good way to clear my head." He pointed his rifle muzzle at the ceiling. "Looks like I'm literally back in the trenches again, though."

A long silence followed, and then Eva spoke. "Thanks for that, Payne, and for being here."

Monroe nodded. "Though I hate to admit it and will deny ever saying it, we wouldn't have gotten this far in finding out what was happening in our own backyard if you hadn't shown up when you did."

He looked into their shadow-laced faces. "Yeah, you would have. You're two of the most capable women I've ever met."

Eva smiled. She got into a crouching position again and pointed her flashlight down the tunnel. "Well, if the meeting of our mutual-admiration society is over, we should get going. It's around ten more minutes to the end."

"And then?" asked Monroe.

"Exactly," replied Payne.

CHAPTER 41

WAGNER LEANED AGAINST THE WALL, HIS BODY RACKED WITH exhaustion and his mind still reeling from the eradication of his colleagues and friends, listening to Bana finish his discussion about his plans for expanding his empire. It was everything he had longed to hear, but then he'd envisioned Elke at his side when the promotion finally came. "A gracious offer to take over your estate in Eastern Europe, sir. I can't thank you enough, but what of you and Alina?"

The two men stepped back as a forklift drove past with another pallet, heading into the freight elevator.

"My wife and I will be relocating to Istanbul to run our new Western Europe office, which will oversee the dissemination of Wayland's wheat imports."

"I thought you said it would be at least six months before this engineered bug completes its toll on the crop storage facilities around the continent?"

Bana nodded. "True, but we need to have the shell corporations in place so the infrastructure is ready when the first shipments of North American wheat from Wayland's warehouses arrive."

Wagner glanced at the lone stairwell that led to the main floor, where Davenport's staff were busy implementing burn protocols on their computers' hard drives since the facility would be shuttered after the last crate of pathogens was removed. "And what about your new business associate...I had the feeling at his office a few days ago that you viewed him as having a limited shelf life."

"Also true but, for now, his supply depots in the US are instrumental. By winter's end, I will determine whether he remains a viable partner or not."

Wagner flipped up the collar on his coat. "I'll head to the roof and check on the men's progress. Is Alina on the bird?"

Bana shook his head. "No, no. She remained in Redding, handling the logistics for getting the goods loaded onto our cargo plane. After that, we'll be wheels up for home and then begin the final phase."

———

PAYNE PULLED BACK from the cobweb-ridden wall vent in the storage area of the basement. The opening was concealed by dozens of crates labeled as scientific equipment. He rested his rifle across his knees as he and the two women mulled over the implications of what they'd just heard.

"This is way bigger than I thought...than even Aaron suspected," whispered Eva. "They're planning to wipe out an entire food source in Europe."

"We need to stop that helicopter from taking off," said Payne.

"First, we have to get past all the people on this level," said Monroe.

He gazed through the wooden louvers on the vent. "Easier said than done, but when you're outnumbered by superior forces, then you need an equalizer. We need to get to their security operations center and get some eyes on what's happening in this building."

"How will that help us down here, exactly?" said Monroe.

"They won't see us coming when we head to the roof and take out that bird."

———

ONCE PAYNE SAW Wagner and Bana go up the stairs, he tore back the insect screening over the vent. He used the noise from the forklifts to blot out his efforts at prying back the old wood grating over the entrance to the tunnel. Once that was complete, he climbed out into the storage room, staying hidden behind some large crates, as the two women followed behind him.

"I doubt the layout is the same since you were here, but I need you to find the breaker box and kill the power in this place," he said to Eva.

She peered out from the side of a crate, glancing around the basement. "This place is nearly three times the size I remember. They did some serious excavation work down here."

Monroe gazed up at the ceiling, pointing to the conduit that ran towards the labs and then snaked around the side, heading into another room. "My money is on that being the utility room."

Payne glanced down at the pistol Eva was clutching with white knuckles. "It's OK. Monroe and I will do the heavy lifting; you just get that power turned off. Chances are that no one will even be inside that room."

Monroe rested her hand on Payne's forearm. "Look, there are probably quite a number of people in here, some of whom might even be locals, and they probably have no idea about Wayland's plans."

"If you're asking me to be selective with a person on the other end of my front sight, I'll do my best. But not if it puts any of us at risk."

"Fair enough," said Monroe.

They waited until the next forklift drove past, then split off into their separate directions, with Eva heading to the left and Payne and Monroe darting to the right towards the passageway that led past the stairs.

Approaching an intersection, Payne stopped at the sound of footfalls heading their way. Monroe came over to his side, both of them pressing against the wall. Payne only waited long enough to see if it was a security guard, and he rushed out, slamming his rifle stock into the side of the guy's head and driving him to the ground.

Once Payne was certain the man was unconscious, he grabbed the keys off his belt.

A door down the hallway opened, and two guards trotted out.

Payne and Monroe both raised their weapons and fired off a burst of rounds from their suppressed rifles, dropping the men on the tiled floor.

Payne moved forward, stepping over the bodies and peering inside the room. "Jackpot."

They both stared inside at dozens of closed-circuit TV monitors that covered the inner and outer regions of the facility.

He motioned for Monroe to watch the hallway while he stepped inside and surveyed the video feeds.

"Looks like they're nearly done stuffing that helicopter with their precious cargo. We need to get to that roof."

The overhead lights in the hallway flickered, then went dark. The emergency lights activated, partially illuminating the room.

"Thank you, Eva. This will give us a slight edge over the guards in here."

Payne moved towards a metal locker mounted on the concrete wall near the door. He pulled out the keys from the guard and fiddled with them until he found the right one.

He swung open the locker, then shot a grin back at Monroe. "Looks like it's time for a weapons upgrade."

He set down his AR rifle and pulled out an MP5, inserting a thirty-round magazine and grabbing two more off the rack inside. He repeated the same motions with a second rifle that he handed off to Monroe. "These will be a lot easier to maneuver with inside this building."

He reached back inside the locker, pulling out a 12-gauge Benelli M4 shotgun. He grabbed a box of slugs, tearing off the side and inserting five slugs into the Benelli. He racked the first slug, then inserted one more before slinging the weapon on his side. "Any sign of Eva?"

Monroe shook her head. "Let's grab her and finish what we came here to do."

They retraced their way back to the stairs, where Eva was waiting. She pointed at the two labs behind her. "There are still hundreds of containers in there, filled with insects."

"We don't have time," said Payne.

"That's what my brother died for. I'm not leaving here without destroying those things."

Before he could respond, Eva turned and walked into the first lab.

Monroe patted her fist on Payne's arm. "Go. I'll stay with her."

Payne bounded up the stairs to the first level, seeing a commotion of movement on the other side of the door as he cracked it open. Peering down the hallway, he noticed numerous employees rushing towards the main entrance.

He continued up the stairs until it ended at the exit door for the roof.

Payne swung open the steel door and rushed out with his MP5 leveled ahead, the intense rotor wash from the helicopter blasting over him.

Rounding the corner of the parapet, he barely saw the tactical baton heading towards his face. Payne thrust up his arms, his right forearm and the MP5 taking the brunt of the strike. The force slammed him back into the wall, the rifle dropping from his grip.

Wagner rushed at him with an overhead strike. Payne angled off to the side, sending a swift low kick into the man's right knee, which buckled. The German swung the baton in an arc, causing Payne to jump back to avoid being struck. Payne reached for his pistol, but Wagner rushed at him again, slamming his shoulder into Payne's ribs, then lifting his head abruptly and smacking Payne on the underside of his chin.

Payne was sure he felt some of his teeth crack, and warm blood trickled down from his lip. He immediately drove all his weight into a downward elbow strike on Wagner's spine, then slammed a knee into the German's face, hearing the snapping of nose cartilage. Wagner tumbled back, springing to his feet and pulling out a six-inch folding knife. The German rushed forward with a straight thrust at Payne's waist.

Payne quickly pivoted to avoid being stabbed while slamming down a hammer fist strike on the back of Wagner's arm.

The German groaned but recovered quickly and feinted left, then slashed horizontally. The blade sliced the air beyond Payne's ear as he ducked. Rain pelted his face, mixing with blood from his split lip. Behind Wagner, the helicopter's rotors cast rhythmic shadows across the roof. Three minutes until takeoff, maybe less.

Wagner pressed forward with a combination of strikes.

Each attack was measured, the work of someone who had spent decades perfecting the craft of killing. Payne caught glimpses of his own training in the German's movements. It was like fighting a darker version of himself.

Wagner rushed in with a straight thrust, his boots losing purchase on the slick roof, which provided Payne with a microsecond of opportunity. He parried the strike and sent a heel stomp into the man's knee, snapping several tendons this time.

Wagner growled, collapsing to one side as Payne sent a roundhouse kick into the back of the German's neck. It sounded like a handful of dry twigs snapping as Wagner's head noodled back, and he dropped to the ground, already dead before he struck the asphalt surface.

———

Monroe accompanied Eva inside the first lab, where the journalist headed to the back of the room, turning on the gas lines for the Bunsen burners. They quickly moved to the next lab and did the same thing.

When they were done, Eva removed a lighter from a desk against the wall. She grabbed a cotton rag from a cabinet and lit it, tossing it on the floor and quickly exiting the room. She slammed her palm against the red knob that closed the vacuum-sealed doors on the lab.

"We should make our way back through the tunnel," Eva said.

Monroe gave a hearty nod, moving back into the main storage area. She caught a blur of movement, but it wasn't in time, and an incoming fist connected straight with her face, sending her to the ground.

Davenport's hulking bodyguard kicked her in the side, sending her into one of the crates. He rushed at Eva, grabbing her throat and driving her back into the wall, lifting her off the ground.

Her eyes widened as she fought to breathe, slamming her hands down on his massive forearms, but to no avail.

———

PAYNE FELT a blast of air from behind as the helicopter engines throttled for lift off. He glanced across the roof, spotting the faces of the Wayland CEO and Wagner's boss, which he'd seen earlier from the basement vents.

He yanked the Benelli shotgun off his back and slid off the thumb safety while focusing the front bead just below the base of the rear rotor. He marched forward, dumping the first round, then racking a new one and firing and repeating as the helicopter started to take off, concentrating his efforts on the quarter panel over the hydraulics. The helicopter lifted off, veering to the left and heading over the treetops. Its ascent only lasted a few minutes as red fluid spewed from the wounded tail section.

The pilot tried compensating, increasing power to the main rotor. The maneuver might have worked in clear weather, but the wind shear coming off the mountains caught the aircraft broadside. Metal screamed as the rear rotor assembly began to disintegrate.

"One more shot for insurance," Payne muttered, racking another slug and sending it downrange.

The helicopter swayed drunkenly, its nose dipping, then rising as the pilot fought for control. Payne could see the two passengers inside the main cabin being thrown against their restraints.

The heavily laden bird careened to the left, then to the right, rapidly descending in a spiral.

The front end connected with the tops of several old pines,

which tore through the metal like it was aluminum foil. The helicopter spun in a circle before impacting an outcropping of basalt and crashing to the ground in flames.

MONROE CURLED ON HER SIDE, coughing while sensing a coppery taste in her mouth. She staggered to her feet, rushing at the brute and sending two right hooks into his kidney region.

It was as hard as she had ever struck a man, but it seemed to have no effect as the maniacal ape turned, striking her in the shoulder with his forearm.

She held up a hand to prevent her face from being slammed into the wall and managed to stay upright this time. Monroe saw Eva's face turning gray as the thug continued to choke the life out of her with his other hand.

The deputy shuffled to the right, yanking a fire extinguisher off the wall and swinging it into the man's lower back. His legs buckled, and his grip on Eva loosened. Monroe swung hard again, this time connecting with the back of his skull. A cracking sound followed, and the man slumped to the side and collapsed as blood drained out from his head.

Eva leaned forward, resting both of her hands on her knees while she gasped for air.

Monroe saw an orange glow reflecting off the walls. Both women pivoted around, seeing flames in the lab licking up the walls. She grabbed Eva's arm and yanked her towards the stairs as both of them raced up onto the main level.

The deputy spun around at the sound of footfalls behind them, relieved to see Payne bounding down the stairs.

"This whole place is gonna blow," Eva shouted, yanking open the door as they flowed into the panicked crowd of staff who were fleeing out the main entrance.

Bursting through the front doors, the three of them veered off to the left towards the farthest parking lot, taking cover behind a dumpster.

A second later, the windows on both floors of the building blew out, followed by a massive ribbon of flames flowing out the front entrance like an orange python trying to escape confinement.

Monroe pointed towards a burning swath of trees beyond the facility. "That your handiwork, Payne?"

He shook his head, looking in the region of the helicopter crash site and then back at the facility. "Our handiwork."

CHAPTER 42

48 HOURS LATER

PAYNE PAID THE MECHANIC FOR HIS MOTORCYCLE REPAIRS AND drove the Indian out of the double-bayed garage, stopping in the corner of the parking lot to transfer his gear from his rental car. Just as he finished, his iPhone buzzed. He pulled it out, seeing it was Alisa.

"You're hard to get ahold of, Kyle. I've been trying for a coupla days."

"Yeah, lots to tell you about sometime. But I've gotta wrap up a few things, and then I'm meeting friends for breakfast, so maybe I can call you this evening."

"Wow, that's amazing."

"What?"

"That you have friends. I mean, besides me."

"Haha."

"I actually have dinner plans tonight, so let me just relay the intel you asked about."

"Fire away."

"So the deputy's brother, Derek Monroe, was in fact a decorated soldier in the Army Rangers, but he didn't die during a deployment."

Payne narrowed his eyes. "How, then?"

"All I can tell you is that I did some prying and located his death certificate online, which was signed by the Absynth County Coroner's Office. He died almost a year ago last week. Cause of death was bludgeoning. He was found in his vehicle on the side of the road. Next of kin was listed as Rebecca Monroe and a T. Larkin."

"Tommy Larkin?"

"I just read what was printed on the form. Monroe is actually listed as family. Larkin is only listed as a close contact, which probably means he's not blood-related."

There was a long moment of silence as Payne scanned the cumulus clouds above for answers. He thought about the cigar stubs on Monroe's porch and her comment about how she and her uncle would hang out there, solving the world's problems, along with how he recalled their close connection during the grueling march from the field station. *Larkin must be family to her.*

"Hey, you still there?"

"Yeah, sorry. Hey, thanks. I'll give you a call sometime this week. Have a good dinner."

"No problem. And I want to hear all the details of your road trip so far. Some of us are stuck indoors all day at real jobs."

He rubbed his sore arm. "Being a full-time nomad is turning into a real job."

"Take care, Kyle."

Payne leaned against his motorcycle, recalling what Monroe had told him about her brother during the drive back to the campground last week.

Hardest part is the not knowing. Derek died a year ago this week, killed who knows where. It's the "where" part that tears me apart, wondering what he was doing during his final moments on this Earth.

"Shit, I assumed he was KIA somewhere overseas, but he died right here, just like Eva's brother," he muttered.

Payne walked back to the garage and handed over the keys to his rental vehicle, then returned to the Indian. He pondered over the revelation about the deputy's brother during the drive to the field station to gather the rest of his items, a part of him hoping he would cross paths with Larkin one last time.

————

Upon arriving, Payne found Larkin sitting on the porch of the dining hall, sharpening an ax with a ceramic stone. Leaning against the wall was the old hunter's weathered rifle that he'd had with him during their frenzied trek along the Beachum Trail.

"That's an interesting caliber," Payne said, settling into the chair beside him. ".264 Winchester. Don't see many of those around anymore."

Larkin's hands stilled momentarily on the ax handle. "Good round for long range. Stable in the winds we get out here."

"Especially in these mountain passes." Payne glanced down at the meadow below. "As I recall there was a case…four cases, in fact, in the past year involving some Filipinos who were gunned down by an unusual caliber in the backcountry." He continued quietly, "All perfectly placed shots, from what I heard. The kind of shooting that takes more than just skill…it takes patience. The patience of someone who's hunted mountain lions for thirty years."

A low row of cumulus clouds scuttled across the valley. Larkin finally looked up, his eyes hard but not hostile. "You've made your point."

"The Filipino workers who killed Derek...you tracked them down one by one. Lured them to a remote canyon."

"That what Monroe thinks?"

"Monroe doesn't want to think about it. But I bet she knows. Just like she knows who's been watching her back all these years."

A long silence stretched between them, filled only by the sound of leaves falling on the metal roof.

Finally, Larkin spoke, his voice low and steady. "Derek was more than just Becky's brother. He was the son I never had. Watched him grow up, taught him about the wilderness, celebrated when he made Ranger." His weathered fingers stroked the hickory ax handle. "Then four of McG's thugs beat him to death over some plants. Left him alongside the road like garbage."

"The law couldn't touch them, or probably even locate them, given their connection to Graves," Payne said. It wasn't a question.

"Oh, Becky and the sheriff tried. But they only prodded so deep. I think they stopped once they saw the direction the investigation was headed." Larkin's eyes met Payne's.

"But sometimes justice needs a long reach," said Payne.

"You would know about that."

Payne nodded slowly. They were two of a kind, in their own way. Men who understood that some debts could only be paid in blood.

"That hunt is finished," Larkin said finally.

"I hope you can find some peace now, though that's often easier said than done." Some secrets, Payne knew, were better left in the wilds.

Payne stood, extending his hand, and the two men shook. "Thank you for letting me stay here. I need to be pushing on, but maybe I'll be able to take that tracking class of yours another time."

"You're always welcome back here, Kyle."

He walked off the porch, heading to his motorcycle.

"Watch yer topknot, as the old mountain men used to say."

"Likewise, Tommy."

CHAPTER 43

PAYNE PULLED HIS MOTORCYCLE UP TO CARO'S CAFÉ AND WAS about to head inside when he saw Monroe making a beeline across the street towards him.

She walked with purpose, suddenly veering towards the edge of the lot, motioning for him to follow.

He trotted up next to her, following her towards an old blue Chevy pickup truck before Paige's pottery shop.

The young woman had just exited the side door, gripping a large plastic tote that she slid into the open bed of the truck.

"Heading out?" Monroe asked.

"Yeah, gotta zip down to Malibu. A friend of mine is opening a new gallery."

"Where's Bosco?" inquired Payne, glancing around the property.

"With my brother in Redding for a while. It's practically his second home."

"Most likely his permanent home from now on," said Monroe, resting her hand on her service pistol. "I know you were Matt Graves' lookout in town. You were the one feeding him info on what was going at our department, along with Payne's and Eva's movements."

Paige scrunched her eyebrows together. "What? That's crazy, Becky. Why in the hell would I do that?"

Monroe thrust her chin at the pottery shop. "Sales have tanked in the past few years. Earl told me you'd brought it up more than a few times to him and how you might have to shut down for good unless something came through."

The deputy stepped closer, causing Paige to back into the passenger door. "Maybe you thought I'd forgotten that you and Graves had a thing back in high school. I had to actually look it up in my old yearbook...the photo of you two together at the homecoming dance. So imagine my surprise when I found multiple calls from you on his cellphone at the gulch, where he tried to kill all of us, Paige." She raised a fist. "He was going to fucking murder all of us and toss our bodies in that canyon."

Monroe was so close to the woman's face that Payne wasn't sure what was about to unfold.

Paige's shoulders slumped, and she moved both her hands to her face, lowering her head. "He told me there'd be a steady paycheck if I just kept an eye on things around here. All I had to do was call him whenever I saw anything unusual. I didn't know what he was doing with the information."

"A drug trafficker with a band of ex-cons and you thought it'd be a good idea to sign on with him. Do you know how many people have died in the past week, Paige?" She grabbed Paige's right shoulder, spinning the woman around and cuffing her hands while reading her rights.

Payne stepped back. "This might be the best part of my day. Certainly the most surprising part."

"Who did *you* think the town snitch was?" asked Monroe

as she gripped Paige's arm and led her across the street to the sheriff's department.

He glanced at the café, grateful to be wrong about his suspicions that Earl was the informant. "Not Paige." He leaned in towards the potter. "I still need to get that ceramic canteen I put on layaway."

Monroe said, "Sorry, everything in her truck, shop, and home is now connected with her case."

Payne hung back, remaining outside as Monroe escorted the woman into the lobby and placed her in the small holding cell as he had a moment of déjà vu.

He saw Eva pull up at the café in her RAV4 and go inside. Payne walked back across the street, heading in and standing beside her in line. "Earl makes a mighty good blueberry Danish," he said.

She chuckled. "I'd meet all of my calorie needs for the week with one of those." Eva glanced around the dining room. "I thought Becky was going to join us before you head out?"

Payne shot his thumb towards the street. "She might be a while. She just hauled off Paige for being McG's informant. Can you believe it?"

Eva shrugged her shoulders. "Damn, I really have been away too long. Never figured Paige to get mixed up with him, but then they did date for a while in high school."

They stepped up to the counter and ordered. "Chai tea and an egg burrito," said Eva.

"And a black coffee and blueberry Danish for Kyle," said Earl.

Payne raised a hand. "Yes on the Danish, but make it two cortados."

Earl smirked. "Is this a joke?"

"Surprised you can even pronounce the name of that drink, Payne," said Eva with a chuckle.

"I'm trying to evolve, alright." Payne tossed down a twenty-dollar bill. "Keep the change."

They moved to a table in the corner. A minute later, the bell on the front door jingled, and Monroe walked in, heading over with a small case under her arm.

She sat down between the two of them, sliding the soft case towards Payne. "Here's your .38 back. Just keep in mind that not every cop in this state will be as lenient about you having this as me."

"Noted." He glanced in the direction of the sheriff's department. "Who's running the shop over there?"

"Well, I am for now. A couple of colleagues of mine from the Weaverville police department have come up to help for a few weeks until we get things figured out."

"Sheriff Rebecca Monroe...that sounds pretty good to me," said Payne.

"Amen," chimed Eva.

"We'll see. I'd sure have some big boots to fill."

"Hanson would be proud of you," Eva said.

"And how's Kessel?" inquired Payne.

Monroe drummed her finger on the edge of the table. "He's out for at least six weeks, and then he'll have to see what his physical therapist says." The deputy sighed. "Other than that, it looks like I'm going to have the presence of the FBI and DEA for the foreseeable future as they comb through Graves' place and what's left of the Wayland property."

"They'll probably be knocking on your cabin door at the field house," said Eva as she glanced at Payne.

"Well, they'll have to catch me when I'm not out on a hike."

"Is that code for you'll be across the Oregon border soon?" said Monroe.

"You have a very active imagination, Deputy." He leaned

back as Earl came with the order, setting down Eva's egg burrito along with the chai tea, followed by Payne's Danish and two cortados.

Payne slid one espresso drink towards Monroe before taking a sip of his own cup. "I'd better not regret this."

Monroe gave him an incredulous look, holding back a grin as she watched him.

Payne set the cup down, biting his lip and narrowing his eyes. "This must be an acquired taste."

Both women snickered, then broke out into laughs.

Monroe rested her hand on his shoulder. "It's alright, Payne. Not everyone is meant for high culture."

He slid his drink towards her. "Enjoy."

The next half hour was filled with recounting their harrowing ordeal during the past few days, followed by their plans for the near future.

Eventually, Eva got up to leave.

"Headed back to LA?" asked Monroe.

Eva pursed her lips, glancing out the window. "To Aaron's old lab by the field station for a while. There's so much of him in there. After that, I think I'll stay at his house and maybe see if Absynth grows on me again. My editor is certainly interested in having me write something up on Theo Davenport and what went on out here at his lab."

"See you around, Eva," said Monroe as the two women embraced.

The journalist moved towards Payne and gave him a hug. "I hope your trip up the coast is uneventful, though it seems like the consulting world is sure harder than I thought."

He laughed, and for the first time since he arrived in Absynth, he felt the tension in his shoulders drain away. "And I hope to read about your Pulitzer one day."

She winked and headed to the door.

They watched her back out and drive off, both of them silent for a few minutes.

"Mind if I ask you something?" inquired Payne. "And if you choose not to answer, there'll be no hard feelings."

She gave him a puzzled look. "What's on your mind?"

"During the drive back to the campground on that first day…when you spoke about your brother's death, I assumed he died during a combat deployment." He gazed into her eyes. "But that's not what happened, is it?"

Monroe stroked the side of her drink, then pushed it away. "No. He, um, was killed right here in his own hometown." She canted her head. "Guy survives getting shot at and blown up for years and then comes back here and meets his end at the hands of a few potheads."

"Graves' men, those four Filipinos who were found dead in the canyons west of here during this past summer?"

She nodded, her eyes moistening. "Not sure how you put all that together, but, yeah. Derek had been gone for a few years, and when he came back during leave, he wanted to find a new swimming spot where he could take his wife and kids on a picnic. He ended up stumbling across one of Graves' latest pot plantations in a small side canyon off Templeton Creek."

"And they couldn't let him get away, especially if they knew who his sister was."

"His body, it was so badly beaten, and he…" She paused, sniffling and holding a hand up to her mouth as she whispered, "His body was found in his truck along the side of the road a day later."

"Just like Aaron's. Is that why you were so skeptical of someone tagging me?"

Monroe nodded. "Same MO. I figured Toko or Graves was sending a message to stay out of the backcountry."

"Hence, 'the Ghost' story. The local news was just playing off an age-old folktale, but it helped brush away suspicion from the actual vigilante." He slid his chair closer, glancing around at the other patrons across the room before he spoke. "Larkin. I saw his rifle and remembered that Dottie said the victims of the Ghost had all been shot with an unusual-caliber rifle."

She leaned back. The look in her eyes was identical to what he'd seen when they were being held at gunpoint at the field station.

"How long have you known it was him?" he asked.

"I wasn't entirely sure until I saw what he did to Graves at that gulch. Or maybe I didn't want to put all the pieces together in case it was Tommy."

"For what it's worth, those four guys got the sentence they deserved, just like Graves." Payne rested his hand on hers. "This secret is safe with me."

Monroe sighed. "Maybe you and I are not so different after all."

He thought about the body count around this town since he arrived and how many more there would have been if not for Monroe's moral compass. "You are what is best in an officer of the law, Becky. I hope you know that."

Payne stood, placing his hand on her shoulder. "I've gotta head out. I just hope I can find a truck stop somewhere on the road north that serves some tar-black coffee."

She chuckled, sliding her hand over his this time. "Safe travels wherever you end up, my friend."

"And I wish you, and the people here, sunnier days ahead." He headed to the door, pausing to wave at Earl.

Once outside, Payne inhaled the fragrance of evergreen trees hanging in the air, then got on his bike and donned his helmet.

After a mile of driving through Absynth, he came to an empty four-way stop and lingered for a moment, gazing at the snowcapped peak of Mount Shasta, then turning north.

He couldn't wait to cross the Oregon state line and camp somewhere on the peaceful shores of the Pacific.

ABOUT THE AUTHOR

Did you enjoy *Blood Trail*? Please consider leaving a review on Amazon to help other readers discover the book.

———

JT Sawyer is the pen name for author Tony Nester who writes survival and vigilante-justice thrillers. Before becoming a full-time writer, JT spent 30 years teaching survival courses in the American Southwest for the military special operations community, at the university level, and for a variety of federal agencies. He also served as a consultant for the film industry and provided training in mantracking and fieldcraft for actors Josh Brolin and Emile Hirsch. Nowadays, JT prefers having a roof over his head and placing his fictional characters in dire straits. He lives with his family and several rescue dogs in Colorado.

———

Want to connect with JT? Visit him at his website:

www.jtsawyer.com

ALSO BY JT SAWYER

Printed in Dunstable, United Kingdom